Dear Reader

'Fish out of water' scenarios are brilliant for either revealing or developing a character. They can show others what they're made of or discover strengths they didn't know they possessed. I used one of these in A FATHER BEYOND COMPARE to give my child-phobic hero, Tom, a chance to learn something about himself when he offers to care for a small boy. This small boy, Mickey, is the son of my heroine, Emma, and I gave both of them a 'fish out of water' scene to start with as well. Or maybe that should be a 'fish *in* water', seeing as I hurled their camper van into a rain-swollen river and then trapped it on debris in the middle of the torrent.

Please let me know if you've enjoyed the kind of drama that my **SERT** series has provided, because I'd love an excuse to revisit this team of emergency response personnel and follow them into the kind of tension that can easily filter into their more private lives.

Happy reading

Alison

This rescue had just become that much more complicated.

He could look into the space that held the driver's seat. A seat that was under water. The driver's back was hunched into the corner of the windscreen, but her upper body was well above the water. Clutched in her arms was a very small boy, who almost disappeared into the protective circle of those slim, bare arms.

Two sets of huge, dark, terrified eyes stared up at Tom.

Tom smiled. 'Good to see you guys,' he said calmly. 'About time we got this spot of bother sorted out for you, isn't it?'

The terror in the larger set of dark eyes changed to something approaching incredulity and then, amazingly, the woman's lips curved into a wide smile. 'Oh, yes…please!'

That smile touched something deep in Tom's heart.

A FATHER
BEYOND COMPARE

BY
ALISON ROBERTS

MILLS & BOON®
Pure reading pleasure

First published in Great Britain 2007
Large Print edition 2007
Harlequin Mills & Boon Limited,
Eton House, 18-24 Paradise Road,
Richmond, Surrey TW9 1SR

© Alison Roberts 2007

ISBN-13: 978 0 263 19363 3

Set in Times Roman 17¼ on 20 pt.
17-0907-48849

Printed and bound in Great Britain
by Antony Rowe Ltd, Chippenham, Wiltshire

Alison Roberts lives in Christchurch, New Zealand. She began her working career as a primary school teacher, but now juggles available working hours between writing and active duty as an ambulance officer. Throwing in a large dose of parenting, housework, gardening and pet-minding keeps life busy, and teenage daughter Becky is responsible for an increasing number of days spent on equestrian pursuits. Finding time for everything can be a challenge, but the rewards make the effort more than worthwhile.

Recent titles by the same author:

ONE NIGHT TO WED*
EMERGENCY BABY*
THE SURGEON'S PERFECT MATCH
THE DOCTOR'S UNEXPECTED PROPOSAL†

Specialist Emergency Rescue Team
†*Crocodile Creek: 24-Hour Rescue*

CHAPTER ONE

IMMINENT disaster could be seen in the rear-view mirror but there was absolutely nothing Emma White could have done to prevent the accident.

Not when it came from behind like that. When she hadn't even *seen* the small truck following her campervan down the long hill towards the bridge.

A one-way bridge.

The signs further up the hill had been perfectly clear. Arrows indicated that the traffic coming from the opposite direction had the right of way on the narrow old wooden bridge that spanned a canyon through which a large river coursed.

Emma had approached with due caution.

She was, after all, in an unfamiliar country, driving a heavy vehicle that required a far greater stopping distance than the compact hatchback she was used to driving. That distance was further compromised today because the roads were still slick after recent rain.

Her caution had been justified. There was a car coming towards them, well over halfway across the bridge and travelling swiftly. Emma was waiting her turn to move. Her hands were on the steering-wheel and, instinctively, when the sharp forward jolt occurred, she pulled down hard on the wheel to try and prevent a head-on collision as her car was shunted towards the oncoming vehicle.

Mickey was sitting in the front seat beside her.

Any mother would have taken the same protective action without thinking.

The jolt had been unexpectedly powerful, however. Forceful enough to jar Emma's foot from its position on the brake. With the wheels now turned away from the road, they were suddenly on the brink of a worse disaster than a head-on collision.

The ground sloped away—too close to the verge of the road. The river snaked along the bottom of a very deep gully and the sides were steep. The bridge had been situated at its narrowest point, which meant there was no margin between the swiftly flowing, rain-swollen river and its banks.

Nowhere for the van to come to rest in relative safety, having careered and then rolled on its enforced detour from the road. The bone-crunching shock of hitting hard ground suddenly changed as the van slipped into the water. But the soft rocking was far from comforting. The van was still moving.

Picking up speed as the current teased and then clutched at a new toy. Filling with icy cold water as the river tried to claim it completely. Being dragged out into a set of boiling rapids.

Being tipped, inexorably, upside down.

'You must be out of your mind!'

'It could work.' Tom Gardiner spoke patiently, not at all surprised by his partner's reaction to the idea.

'No way. It's far too dangerous.'

'It's a calculated risk. I'm prepared to take it.'

'It's not justified, mate. They're probably dead, anyway.'

The two men, both paramedics attached to SERT—Specialist Emergency Response Team—peered down from the hovering helicopter.

It certainly appeared pointless to risk their own lives to help the victims involved in this scenario. Way below them, towards the middle of the swift and rain-swollen river, they had a clear view of the reason they'd been scrambled. A campervan had apparently missed a sign informing the driver to give way on a single-lane bridge and had careened off the road. The van had been swept far enough into the canyon to make access virtually impossible from the ground.

The tangle of debris that had caught the van's chassis and halted its journey included some hefty logs but it was on the edge of a strong current. At any moment it could be caught and pulled clear to tumble and roll in the deadly river on its seaward path. The distance it had already travelled made the survival of its occupants debatable but the fact that it was still afloat enough to roll if it did swivel clear of the obstruction was uppermost in Tom's mind as he surveyed the scene.

'They've still got a fair bit of air in there. They could be alive.'

'It's only the side door that's accessible. If they've got their safety belts on they'll be long gone. The driver must be completely under water.'

'Maybe not. We don't know how long it's been that far under.'

'The witness said it was rolling in the water.'

'He also said he thought he saw a woman and a child in the front.' Tom was getting impatient. He leaned further out the side door, blinking as enough of a blast of icy air sneaked around the edge of his helmet visor to make his eyes water. He twisted his head to keep the target in view as the helicopter did another slow circle. 'I'm going down to check.'

'And what happens if you do find someone alive?'

'I'll get them out.'

'No. You'd try and get them out and probably join them in the ride downstream. We can't attach a winch line to keep that thing stable, Tom.'

'I know that.'

'And there's no way of getting a line out from shore. The fire boys haven't arrived yet. And we'll need some boats and divers on scene.'

'It's going to be too late by then.' Under normal circumstances Tom was inclined to err on the cautious side himself but the fact that there could be a woman and child involved here made it seem like a copout to be cautious. 'I can at least go down for a look. If there's no sign of life, it'll take the urgency out of things a bit. What do you say, Terry?'

The pilot of the rescue chopper had worked with SERT for years now. A lot longer than Tom's relatively new partner. Tom not only trusted the pilot's opinion regarding any safety issues in the air, he knew he would get the encouragement he needed to go the extra mile to help someone in dire need. The middle-aged pilot had just become a grandfather. He was a soft touch.

'Go for it,' Terry said. 'Winch conditions are good. Just don't attach us to anything down there. I don't fancy getting my feet wet.'

Neither did Tom but that was exactly what happened as he neared his descent target. His boots dragged in the surface of the river and filled with icy water.

'Hey, I said minus two, not ten!' he complained to Josh via the helmet radio. 'I've got wet feet!'

'Sorry, mate.'

'Take me up a bit and then see how close we can get. I can't see a thing yet.'

Except for the ominous speed that made the eddies around the pile of debris look like white-water rapids. And the deep grey-green that advertised the depth of the river channel that was running alongside the obstruction.

The big square white van had an incongruously cheerful rainbow stripe painted along its side. It was bobbing slowly but something underneath—the front axle, maybe—had caught firmly on a thick branch. That branch belonged to a large tree that the earlier storm must have uprooted.

'Looks reasonably stable,' Tom relayed. 'I want to stand on the side door and see if I can get a view into the front compartment.'

From where he was hanging now, he could see the passenger's side window and a portion of the windscreen. The side window was shut tightly but light reflecting on the glass made it impossible to see through. The nose of the vehicle pointed down and another log was jammed against the front door. Even if there was someone trying to open that door from the inside, it would be a pointless struggle.

The roar of the helicopter drowned out the sound of rushing water as Tom drifted slowly sideways but he could feel the cold spray of wind-whipped water on his cheeks. His feet touched the side of the van and he bounced slightly as it bobbed. He shook his head to clear droplets of water from his visor, leaning forward, trying to see into the side window at least.

And then he saw it.

A hand. Pressed against the glass. Small fingers that seemed to try and then fail to find something to hold onto.

A child's fingers.

A child who was still alive.

'Contact,' Tom said tersely. 'We've got a live one here.'

'Hell!'

Tom wasn't sure if it was Josh or Terry who expressed the frustration they now all faced of trying to do anything more in the immediate stage of this rescue mission. What on earth could they do?

If the van had been stable, they could have winched the victims up to the helicopter, but when the van could be swept away at any moment, it was far too dangerous to have a line that could potentially pull the chopper down.

How long would it take the fire trucks to arrive? The land-based teams had been dispatched at the same time as the SERT paramedics but they had to travel a long way by road. The fire service appliances had the lines to secure an unstable vehicle but someone would have to abseil down the side of the gully to get near the water. The boat rescue team would also be needed. And the team of police divers in case it all went wrong.

It would all take far too long.

'I'm unhooking,' Tom informed his colleagues.

'Tom! No!'

It was too late. Tom had snapped open his winch hook as he'd spoken and he now held the line out to one side, signalling for Josh to retract it. A muttered curse echoed in his helmet from above but the line snaked upwards out of harm's way.

The smooth side of the van was now a skating rink. Sleek wet metal that tipped gently one way and then another. Tom dropped to his knees as he felt himself sliding, his gloved fingers sweeping in a rapid arc to catch the handle of the door to the back compartment.

And then he was lying flat on the side of the van, aware of the tense silence within his helmet and the sound of the helicopter outside it, hovering as its crew watched with trepidation. Were they already planning to follow Tom's path downriver when he got swept away? Hoping he might get to shore at a point where they could winch him back to safety?

He wasn't going to get swept away, dammit. Not before he'd checked out the owner of those small fingers anyway. With an immense effort he dug his fingers behind the handle and pulled, heaving the door outwards.

It opened. The door snapped back and Tom slid far enough to touch a wing mirror with his boot. The metal attachment was fortunately strong enough to take his weight and, using it as an anchor, Tom was able to pull himself back by gripping the top edge of the door. And then he could see inside the compartment.

The water level came at least halfway up and the surface was awash with debris. Clothing. Cooking utensils. Maps. And…a teddy bear.

Ignoring the mental alarms sounding stridently, Tom twisted his body, hooking his legs into the gap he had created in the side of the vehicle.

And then he slid inside the floating camper-van. As his feet found a solid point well beneath the water level he pulled the door closed again behind him in the hope of preventing the swirl of disturbed water outside filling any more of the interior.

With a silent prayer to whatever forces might have the power to keep the van exactly where it was for the time being, Tom manoeuvred himself to face the front of the vehicle.

'Hello,' he called. 'My name's Tom and I'm here to help. Can anyone here me?'

'Yes!' The sound was somewhere between a word and a sob. A feminine sound. 'Help us… Please!'

'That's what I'm here for.' Tom took a slow step through the thigh-deep water, no longer aware of the chill. Between the front seats of the van was a window-like gap in the wall that separated the seats from the back compartment. Light from outside made that gap glow in comparison to the gloom of the space Tom was in. It also made it easy to head in the right direction.

'What's your name? Are you injured?'

'I'm…Emma.'

'And you've got someone with you?'

'Just my son…Mickey.'

The owner of those small fingers, then. 'Hey, Mickey,' Tom called. 'How're you doing?'

The only response was an adult groan. 'Don't try and stand on me again, Mickey. It… hurts…'

'Sorry, Mummy.'

'Are you injured, Emma?' Tom pushed a sodden pillow to one side as he took another step forward.

'I'm…not sure.'

Both Emma and her son had an intriguing accent. An appealing, soft lilt that evoked an image of something British. Possibly rural. The fact that these people were in a foreign country triggered something else protective in Tom. They would be terrified in any case but being away from home had to make this all that much worse.

'What's hurting, Emma?'

'My foot mainly…it's kind of trapped under something. And my leg. The steering-wheel's sort of bent.'

Tom groaned inwardly. This rescue had just become that much more complicated. Any visions he'd had of balancing on the side of the van and miraculously being able to get the victims winched to safety before land-based back-up arrived went out the window. Trying to do an extrication on a trapped person in this vehicle was going to need back-up in spades. And even then it was going to be dodgy.

He had reached the gap in the wall. He could look into the space that held the driver's seat. A seat that was under water. The driver appeared to in a crouched position, her back hunched into the corner of the windscreen but her upper body was well above the water. Clutched in her arms was a very small boy who almost disappeared into the protective circle of those slim, bare arms.

Two sets of huge, dark, terrified eyes stared up at Tom.

Tom smiled. 'Good to see you guys,' he said calmly. 'About time we got this spot of bother sorted out for you, isn't it?'

The terror in the larger set of dark eyes changed to something approaching incredulity and then, amazingly, the woman's lips curved into a wide smile. 'Oh, yes…please!'

That smile touched something deep in Tom's heart. This was one brave lady. Maybe it was a front to try and reassure her small son but that didn't make it any less courageous. And courage was a quality that Tom valued very highly.

He smiled at the small boy. 'G'day, Mickey. How old are you, mate?'

'Go away,' Mickey told him. 'I don't like you.' He burst into tears.

'It's all right, honey.' Emma's grip on her son tightened noticeably but Tom could see the grimace of pain as Mickey wriggled. 'Tom's here to rescue us. It's all right. Remember your manners.'

'But I can rescue you, Mummy. I was going to open the door but I'm too short and I don't want to stand on your sore bits again.'

'No, don't stand on Mummy's sore bits,' Tom said hurriedly. 'I know I look a bit scary, Mickey, but I am here to help. You and Mummy. Do you have any sore bits?'

'No.' Mickey's face turned from where it was buried against his mother's neck. 'I'm four.'

Tom blinked, trying to make the connection, but then realised Mickey was answering a much earlier question.

'Wow. You're old.'

'I'm not old. I'm big.'

'Mmm.' Tom was happy to agree. He needed to win this child's trust—as quickly as possible. A plan was formulating in his head as he used the time this conversation was taking but it was hard to try and sound relaxed. 'Are you here on holiday with Mummy?'

'We're having an adventure.'

'You sure are,' Tom agreed dryly. 'I'm sure you didn't plan to have this bit of it, though.'

Mickey screwed his face up into lines of deep consideration. 'No. This was a *nanksident.*'

'Do you remember what happened?' Tom was leaning in more closely now. He could feel the edge of the wall digging into his abdomen as he peered down. He didn't want to frighten Mickey by reaching an arm in just yet. A terrified and uncooperative child could ruin what he was planning before it even became a possibility. He also wanted to check Emma out. Right now he was trying to see how well she was able to breathe but Mickey's small body made it difficult to assess the movement of her chest wall to get an impression of a respiration rate. His question was designed to try and find out whether either of these victims had been knocked unconscious at any point.

'There was a *big* bump,' Mickey told him. 'And Mummy said we turned into a boat.'

'There was a bridge,' Emma said. 'One lane. And there was…a car coming…so I stopped.'

'You stopped?' Tom was noting how many words per breath Emma was managing, which seemed to indicate at least some degree of respiratory distress. He couldn't help the note of surprise in his own voice. That wasn't what the witness had told the emergency services.

'Of course I stopped.' Emma was indignant. This was good. A seriously injured person wouldn't have the energy to sound that indignant. 'Do I look like some sort of idiot?'

'No.' Tom's response was rapid. And sincere. Even with thoroughly wet hair plastered in dark strands around an overly pale face, Tom could see fine features and bright eyes that advertised intelligence.

'We got bumped,' Mickey added. 'I told you that.'

Tom was clearly the idiot here but he needed to clarify the information. 'From behind?'

'Yes.'

'Josh?' Tom's query was brief. 'You hearing any of this?'

'Enough,' came the response from within his helmet. 'Will pass it on to the cops.'

'Who's Josh?' Emma asked.

'My partner. He's up in the helicopter, waiting for me to get you out.'

'Waiting for you to get out more likely,' came Josh's voice. 'Get a move on, Tom.'

'How on earth are you going to get us out?'

'I'll take Mickey first.' Tom had to hope he'd won a level of trust by now. 'You want to go for a ride, Mickey?'

'No.'

'You have to, sweetheart.' Emma spoke urgently. 'It'll be my turn after you.' Those huge eyes were on Tom now and the silent plea was heartbreaking. Emma was far from stupid. She knew how much danger they were all in and how much harder it was going to be to rescue her. Tom could actually feel her gathering her determination to save her child. She spoke even more firmly. 'Mickey? Listen to me, darling. You have to do exactly as you're told.'

'But—'

'No buts. You do what Tom tells you to do or I'm going to have to get cross.'

'Can you stand up, Mickey?' Tom tried to sound encouraging. 'Carefully, though, so you don't hurt Mummy.'

'No-o-o.' The small face was as frightened as the voice.

'It's a bit hard for…him to stand up.' Emma had a distinct wobble in her voice now.

'My legs only work *sometimes,*' Mickey said.

Tom frowned, trying to assimilate the new information. Mickey had said nothing hurt but he did seem very small for his age.

'Disability?' he queried succinctly.

'Mild spina bifida,' Emma responded. 'Just starting to walk…with callipers.'

'Anything else I should know?'

Emma shook her head. 'Other than no leg strength, he's perfect. Aren't you, darling?'

This time the smile wasn't for Tom. It was for a child who was very clearly deeply loved. Emma was pressing a kiss to Mickey's wet head and Tom could see the way she screwed her eyes shut, forcing back tears.

'No problem, then.' Lower-limb weakness wouldn't make any difference as far as rescuing Mickey went. And Tom wouldn't have to worry about being kicked in the shins by a terrified child. He leaned further into the compartment. 'Just put your arms up, Mickey. I'm going to pick you up.'

Emma had to peel two small arms from

around her neck. 'Be a good boy,' she told Mickey. 'Love you.'

'I love you, too, Mummy.'

Mickey was sobbing but he held his arms up to Tom. It wasn't hard to pick the small child up but easing the burden through the gap was a little trickier. The van rocked and a dreadful scraping noise could be heard as it moved against the logs.

'*Mummy!*' Mickey wailed.

'It's all right,' Tom said loudly. 'Just hang on, Mickey.' He poked his head back through the gap just for a second. 'I'll be back very soon,' he told Emma.

'Just look after Mickey.' Emma couldn't hold back a sob. 'Please.'

Tom took a step through water that was several inches deeper than when he had gone the other way only minutes before.

'Josh? Send the nappy harness down, mate. Pronto.'

'You know what you're doing, Tom?'

Tom grinned. 'Hope so.'

It was a hair-raising operation. Tom had to

hold a terrified and wriggling child as he opened the side door. Mickey's legs might be hanging rather limply but he was making up for the physical deficit with a wiry little upper body and two very active arms. Tom found a foothold on a part of one of the bunk beds that allowed him to stand just half out of the van. It wasn't until he saw that the winch line was within reach that he started the most dangerous part of his plan.

With Mickey firmly grasped under one arm, he climbed onto the side of the van, grabbed the hook and clipped it on. Mickey was struggling too hard to try and put his legs into the nappy harness and it would have been too big for him anyway, so Tom just held him even more securely.

'Bring us up, Josh.'

As his feet left the side of the van and they dangled in mid-air, the terror was enough to make Mickey go limp all over, apart from two small arms that were wound so tightly around Tom's neck that it was hard to breathe. It proved a problem when they reached the open door of the helicopter and Josh leaned out to take the child. Mickey wouldn't let go.

'I've got to go and get Mummy,' Tom shouted into the small ear. 'You have to go with Josh.'

There was no time to try and reassure him. This was a dodgy enough transfer anyway when there was no extra line to protect the child. Tom held his breath as he felt his partner's hands take hold of Mickey. He had to let go and hope that his precious burden made it safely into the interior of the helicopter. His heart was still pounding as he saw Josh deposit the child into a seat and try to shorten a safety harness enough to be useful.

'Mickey's got spina bifida, Josh. Any lower-limb paresis is normal.' He leaned back on the skid. 'Let's move. Winch me down again.'

'ETA for the boats and fire crews is only ten minutes, Tom. Wait for back-up.'

'No.' Looking down between his feet, Tom could see that the van's position had altered slightly. 'This won't take long.'

How much had Josh and Terry overheard through his communication equipment? Did they know that Emma was trapped? Had they noticed the change in the van's position on the debris?

Was he mad to even think of going back? Of course he was. But Tom could see Mickey staring at him and he could only think of the larger version of those terrified dark eyes. Of a brave young mother who was alone and praying for rescue right now.

He tried to keep his tone upbeat. 'Can't leave a job half-done,' he said. 'And if the boats are on the way you probably won't even need to winch me back up.'

'Wind's come up a bit,' Terry said. 'I'm not sure about this, Tom.'

'We've done it once. We can do it again.'

'You really sure you want to try?'

Tom looked at Mickey again. Then he looked down at the swirling river and the van that contained his mother.

'Oh, yeah…I'm sure.'

Terry grunted. Josh shook his head as he turned to the winch control panel and his voice sounded resigned.

'Checking winch power. Clear skids.'

Terry's permission was equally reluctant but it came nonetheless a second later.

'Clear skids.'

With a final glance and a thumbs-up signal for the tiny boy looking lost inside an adult-sized harness, Tom began his second descent.

Looking way downriver from the vantage point of his altitude, Tom could see vehicular activity on a stony shore where the canyon widened again. Red and blue lights flashed and figures could be seen emerging from the four-wheel-drive rescue Jeeps. Large black rafts were carried on trailers.

They weren't even in the water yet but at least they were nearby. If the worst happened and the van got swept away, Tom would just have to find a way to free Emma and then keep her afloat until a boat reached them. It wasn't an impossible task.

It couldn't be.

Unhooking his winch cable as his feet touched the side of the van felt no less horrible despite the practice run. The metal seemed more slippery and the van less stable. Tom's fingers missed the handle on the first sweep and he was aware of a very unfamiliar sensation too close to panic. It was impossible to take a deep breath to steady himself with the amount of water splashing around him. If he missed the handle on the second try he would have to aim for the wheel and his weight on that might be enough to tip them all towards disaster.

When he caught the handle and the door slid open of its own accord Tom realised just how much the van's position had changed and there was no relief to be found in gaining access. Had Emma managed to keep her head above the water level? Was she still conscious?

'Emma! Can you hear me?' Tom waded through the water and debris, almost falling in his haste to reach the gap. He ignored the rocking of the vehicle—the silence he could detect around him was far more ominous.

'Emma!'

CHAPTER TWO

SHE was so cold. Emma had never been this cold in her entire life. She had never been this terrified. She could ignore the deep ache in her leg, even dismiss the sharp pain in her ribs when she tried to take a deeper breath but she couldn't escape the terror.

Not while she was alone like this, anyway. It had almost gone for a while back there— when Tom had been with them. Having Mickey to focus on had been an overwhelming distraction as well. How long had it been since Tom had taken her son away? Five minutes? Forty-five minutes? Impossible to tell.

At least her teeth weren't chattering hard enough to feel like they were going to shatter now. And her head was still above water, although every so often the van rocked enough to make a wave lap against her face. Emma had to screw her eyes tightly shut when that happened and hold her breath. And pray that Mickey, at least, had made it to safety.

This was all so unfair. So stupid! What right had she to drag her son off on what was probably a wild-goose chase? She could have stayed where she was and come to terms with always having that shadow hanging over her life. She could have kept them both safe. Her parents had thought she was wasting her money.

'Have a holiday closer to home, for goodness' sake,' her mother had said more than once. 'There's absolutely no point in going all the way to New Zealand. He could have found you last year, you know—if he'd *really* wanted to.'

Spain would have been nice. Or the south of France. Or a Greek island. A nice short plane ride away from Wales. Mickey could have built sandcastles while Emma lazed on a beach and tried to sort out the direction she wanted to take at this crossroads in her life.

Instead, she was trapped in a van. Waiting to

be swept to her death. Or maybe to drown first, the way the van was rocking and sending water over her face right now. Either way she was going to die. Alone.

No. Emma took a gasping breath in between the waves. She wasn't going to give up. She was only twenty-eight, for God's sake, and she had a young child who depended on her.

And…and she wasn't alone. She could hear someone yelling her name.

'Tom? Is that you?' Emma opened her eyes and thoughts of imminent death faded. She couldn't see much of the paramedic's face, what with the helmet and visor and a microphone attachment but she could see enough. Dark eyes that were fastened on her. And a smile that could light the darkest of places.

Even the place they were both in right now.

'How it's going, then?'

Such a silly question but Emma was so relieved to see Tom that she had to smile. Then she had an important question of her own. 'Mickey?'

'He's safe. On board the chopper and they'll

be taking him to the ambulance crew to get checked out.'

'Was he…good? No trouble?'

Tom was grinning. 'I only got pinched a few times. He didn't want to leave his mum.'

Emma couldn't hold the tears back. Relief vied with panic that she would never see her child again.

'Hey…' Tom was squeezing himself as far through the gap as he could without falling on top of Emma. 'It's going to be all right. We'll get you out of here in no time.'

She believed him. Almost. 'But my foot's still stuck.'

'I'm going to see if I can do something about that. How are you feeling otherwise?' Tom stripped off a glove and reached down to take hold of her wrist. 'You're pretty cold, aren't you?'

He was taking her pulse. Although her hands were almost numb with the cold, Emma could feel the contact. The warmth of another human touching her. The fear of dying alone evaporated. Even the fear of dying at all faded. If anyone could get her out of this, it would be this big man, with his reassuringly calm manner and that wonderful smile.

'Are you having any trouble breathing?'

'It hurts a bit. I think my ribs got a bit bruised by the steering-wheel.'

'How's your neck? And your head?'

'Fine…I think.'

'Were you knocked out?'

'No.'

'Do you know what day it is?'

'Um…Wednesday.' Tom was trying to assess her level of consciousness. 'The fourteenth,' she supplied. 'We came over on the ferry from North Island yesterday…and we were taking a roundabout route to get to Christchurch.'

'Where are you from?'

'Wales.'

Tom was grinning again. 'Can you sing?'

Emma actually laughed. 'Not right now.'

'Fair enough.' Tom leaned further in. Emma could have wrapped her arms around his neck if she'd wanted to. And she did want to. Very much.

'I'm just going to have a feel down your leg,' Tom told her.

'OK.'

'I hope you don't say that to every man you've just met.' It was astonishing how Tom could actually make a joke of trying to assess how badly she was trapped. It was a great technique, though. Emma trusted him completely. She would do whatever she had to do to be co-operative.

'Ow!'

'Sorry. You've got some trauma. You're bleeding a bit.'

Emma had heard that kind of understatement from medical professionals more than once.

'I do feel pretty weird. Have I lost enough to be in shock, do you think?' Dark eyes flicked up to meet hers and Emma smiled wryly. 'I'm a nurse,' she told Tom. 'I've probably imagined the worst-case scenario here in lurid detail.'

'I'll bet.' Tom was pulling at something well below the water line. Emma felt something metallic scraping against her leg and bit her lip to prevent crying out and restricting his efforts. 'What kind of nursing?'

'I used to be a theatre nurse. I've worked in Emergency, too, and loved that. I've just been a general practice nurse since Mickey was born and I'm more than ready for a change.'

'Not exciting enough?'

'No.'

'So you came looking for some adventure.' Tom grunted with the effort of trying to bend something from his upside down position.

'Not this kind.'

'Long way to come.' Tom adjusted his position. He used one hand to anchor himself on the doorhandle just behind Emma's head and twisted, pushing his other arm further into the water. 'Have you got family in New Zealand?'

Did Mickey's father count? 'Not exactly.'

'Friends?'

'Um…' What she and Simon had had could hardly be described as 'friendship'. A wild affair with undying passion declared on both sides. Something that had ignited so quickly it had bypassed anything resembling a friend-ship. A conflagration that had been over even more quickly than it had begun.

'Not really,' Emma told Tom.

'You don't sound too sure.'

'Mmm.' That was it in a nutshell, wasn't it? Emma wasn't sure. 'It's a bit complicated.'

'Ah-h…' Tom sounded sympathetic but polite. He was still trying to bend whatever piece of metal was trapping Emma's leg. He was also clearly trying to distract her with some conversation but didn't want to tread on any ground that was too personal. 'So you were heading for Christchurch?'

'Yes.'

'My home town.'

'Really?' Why did that suddenly make the largest city in South Island a much more attractive destination?

'Yep.' Tom grunted with the effort he was putting into trying to shift the piece of metal. 'Not necessarily a tourist Mecca, though. How come you're not heading for Queenstown or Milford?'

'Mickey's father lives in Christchurch.'

'Oh…' The sound carried a wealth of understanding this time. Too much. 'He must be looking forward to seeing you guys.'

'He doesn't know we're coming.' Emma wasn't sure why she was blurting out so much information here. Maybe her fear was still too real. If she didn't make it, someone would have to take responsibility for getting Mickey back to his grandparents.

'You're separated?' Tom looked up for an instant which gave the impression he was particularly interested in her response.

'We were never together.'

'Oh…right.' Tom bent his head again. Emma could feel his hand on her leg, searching for a better position to tackle the obstacle. She could also feel his puzzlement.

Of course they had been together. Mickey's conception had hardly been immaculate, had it?

'I ended the relationship,' Emma explained, 'the day I found out I was pregnant with Mickey.'

Tom's face appeared even more swiftly. 'You mean he doesn't know about Mickey yet?'

Emma could sense his disapproval. As though she had disappointed him on some level involving honesty or morality. The need to defend herself was the best distraction he'd come up with so far.

'Simon hadn't seen fit…to tell me that he was married,' she informed Tom. 'So I didn't really feel he was automatically entitled to the truth from me.'

Funny how being faced with the possibility of losing her life hadn't made the guilt go away. In fact, it had just grown stronger, inexplicably fed by the sense of disapproval from a man who was a complete stranger. A stranger she was dependent on if she was going to make it out of this.

Maybe she could help him understand.

'Have you got kids, Tom?'

'Hell, no!' The sound Tom made could only be described as a relieved chuckle. 'I've managed to avoid them so far.'

So he didn't like children, this hero who had just saved her own child? She was curious that the information should seem so disappointing but he *had* saved Mickey so Emma decided she should just feel grateful. He was risking his own life again to try and save her and there was no amount of gratitude that could ever encompass that. Especially when success was far from guaranteed.

As if to emphasise the point, the van suddenly moved. It rocked and then twisted and Emma cried out in alarm. The cry changed to a choking sound as water broke over her face and for a few moments Emma lost her focus on what was happening. Panic clawed at her and she struggled, aware of a sharp pain in her foot and a vice-like grip around her upper body.

'Emma! *Emma!* Try and hold still for just a bit longer. We're almost there.'

How many times had Tom repeated his command before the words made sense? Before Emma stopped coughing and spluttering and struggling to try and escape?

'I'm …sorry,' she finally sobbed. 'I'm just so *scared.*'

'I know.' Tom's words were clipped enough

for Emma to realise that she wasn't the only one scared by the new movement of the vehicle.

'You should get out...while you still can, Tom.'

'No way, babe. We're getting out of this together.' He was pulling at her foot. It hurt like hell but Emma tried to help, pulling as hard as *she* could.

'Try turning your foot,' Tom instructed. 'We're almost—'

His words were cut off as the van shifted again. This time it rolled sideways far enough to put Emma's head right under water. For one paralysing moment she couldn't think of anything more than the horror of drowning.

Then she felt that strong grasp still holding her leg. She remembered the last words she'd heard and twisted her leg, pushing instead of pulling at her foot.

And something moved. Her foot was free. Her leg was being dragged upwards, away from the crumpled compartment. Emma's whole body was moving upwards and for a moment her head was above water again. Just long enough to gulp in a lungful of air and to realise that Tom was trying to move her through the window gap into the back of the van. To where the side door was that he'd entered.

But was that still above water?

Emma had lost all sense of direction. All sense of time. Her body was ahead of her brain in shutting out the horror and her limbs felt heavy and lifeless. Powerless to assist Tom in any way, Emma just floated, aware of nothing but the strength of the arms holding her so tightly and the determination she could feel emanating from the owner of those arms.

If they could survive by sheer willpower, Tom was providing more than enough for both of them.

Emma was dimly aware of being outside the van because an icy wind sent an unbelievable chill right into the marrow of her bones and the noise from the helicopter hovering close overhead was deafening.

Tom was shouting but the instructions didn't seem to be for her, which was just as well because Emma's lips were too numb to move.

Her eyelids drooped and she knew that the effort of trying to open them again would be too great. And maybe that was just as well because the image being cut off was that of the vehicle she'd just been trapped inside.

Somehow they were above it now but still very, very close. Close enough to be bumped and swayed as the van tilted sharply and then swung out into the whirls of the river's main current, with only its tyres visible.

Even the noise and shouting faded then but Emma clung to the sensation that was the only thing of importance.

The security of the arms still around her.

Holding her.

Keeping her alive.

Tom felt the instant that Emma went completely limp in his arms and something akin to anger took hold.

Had he just gone through the most dangerous rescue mission of his career only to fail? There had been no time to even assess the degree of trauma Emma had suffered to her lower leg. What if that piece of twisted metal had been tamponading an arterial bleed and he hadn't had the opportunity to prevent her bleeding to death in the tense minutes of getting her out of the van and winched up to the helicopter?

Time slowed and it seemed to take for ever to get her on board the aircraft and then to get himself inside. In less than a minute Terry had the chopper on safe ground but Tom was barely aware of landing. He was crouched over Emma, tilting her head back to ensure her airway was open. Trying to assess whether or not she was still breathing.

Josh was filling the rest of the space in the cabin.

'Carotid pulse,' he said, 'but no radial. What's your estimation of blood loss?'

'Too much.' Tom could see fresh blood loss on the shredded denim of Emma's jeans. He didn't need to remind Josh of the urgency of controlling the haemorrhage. His partner was already ripping open dressing and bandage packages.

Tom pulled down an oxygen mask and flicked

the flow to full bore. He put the mask on Emma's face and eased the elastic behind her head.

'It's OK,' he told her. 'We're safe now, Emma. You're going to be fine.'

Her face was deathly pale, framed by the long, wet tresses of dark hair.

'She's hypothermic,' Tom warned Josh. 'I'll get a cardiac monitor on.'

'Can't feel any broken bones here.' Josh was taping the pressure bandage in place on Emma's leg. 'Could be just soft-tissue injury. How's her breathing?'

'Shallow,' Tom responded. 'But chest wall movement looks equal.' He had been waiting for the rotors of the helicopter to slow enough to make using a stethoscope useful. 'Sounds clear enough,' he reported moments later.

'Could be some abdominal trauma.' Josh had cut the top of Emma's jeans with shears and pulled the rest of her shirt clear. Tom felt his heart sink as he saw the ugly purple mark marring an expanse of perfect pale skin. If Emma had ruptured her spleen on top of losing blood from the injury to her leg, they may well be too late in starting a fight to prevent her slide into irreversible shock.

Fluids were needed, stat. Wide-bore lines—one in each arm. Pressure cuffs to get the fluid where it was urgently needed—to pump up blood volume and keep enough oxygen circulating to prevent cellular death.

She also needed rapid transport to hospital. The rotors of their aircraft were still turning as Terry kept the helicopter idling. As soon as he and Josh were happy that Emma was stable, they would take off again. With fluids running and the cardiac monitor revealing an overly rapid but normal pattern, take-off was only seconds away.

There had been another reason for landing near the collection of emergency vehicles dotting the lip of the river canyon, however.

'We need to get the kid,' Tom reminded Josh.

'But he's fine,' Josh responded. 'Not a scratch on him apparently. He could go by road.'

'No.' Tom shook his head. 'Mickey needs to come with Emma.'

What if she regained consciousness *en route*

and the distress at having been separated from her child worsened the situation? If Tom had needed any persuasion to stick to his preferred option, it came when Emma's head rolled to one side and then back again. Her eyelids fluttered open and an arm trailing an IV line was raised as her hand reached towards Tom.

'Mickey…'

It was the only word Emma uttered but it was more than enough for Josh to nod agreement. He climbed out the rear door and was back in a very short time with a tiny boy clutched in his arms.

'Mickey's here,' Tom told Emma. 'He's coming with us.'

'Mummy!'

The word was lost in engine noise but it was easy to lip-read. Even easier to read the joy of reunion on that small face. Mickey was actually grinning as he caught sight of his mother. Way too small to match those huge, dark eyes and with a now nearly dry mop of tousled, black curls, Mickey had to be the cutest kid Tom had ever seen.

'Mummy's asleep just now,' he shouted carefully. 'She's not feeling too well and we're going to have another ride in the helicopter so that we can take her to the hospital.'

Fear clouded the dark eyes now and Mickey's bottom lip trembled. How much did the boy understand? With his disability, it was possible that the boy had had quite a lot of experience of hospitals. Maybe enough to know that some people who went into one never came out again?

'Mummy's going to be fine,' he added firmly. 'This is just another part of your adventure, OK?'

That earned him a suspicious stare and the reminder that Mickey had already declared his dislike of Tom. Still, the child made no protest as Josh strapped him into the seat. The extra passenger made it more awkward to work around Emma but it was a short trip of less than thirty minutes and Emma remained stable.

Better than stable, in fact. With at least the external bleeding controlled and rapid infusion of fluids, Emma's level of consciousness improved steadily. By the time she was lifted from the stretcher to the bed in the resuscitation area of the emergency department under the watchful gaze of the assembled trauma team, Emma was awake.

'Mickey,' she said anxiously. 'Where's my son?'

'He's being taken care of.' The doctor in charge of Emma's airway leaned over her reassuringly. 'Don't worry. We need to focus on you for a little while.'

There had been no chance to complete any of the paperwork a job like this generated but, having given all the information he could during the patient handover, Tom was only to happy to use the task as an excuse to stay in Resus, taking over an out-of-the-way corner of a bench.

He had to move a couple of times, to go behind the reinforced glass as X-rays were taken. He was still there when the ultrasound technician arrived with the equipment needed to examine Emma's abdomen.

Josh appeared right behind the bulky machine.

'I've got a date tonight, mate. If I'm late again, I'm going to be in big trouble. You're finishing the paperwork, aren't you?'

'Yeah. I just wanted to find out what the verdict is on Emma's leg. There's a surgical consult that shouldn't be too far away.'

'That'll take hours. You know what it's like around here. They haven't even started that ultrasound.' Josh gave Tom a curious glance. 'If you're that keen on following up, why don't you drop back in on your way home? *After* we've signed off.'

Tom could understand his partner's eagerness. They were at the end of four days of active duty and about to start their four days off. He was looking forward to the time off himself but he hadn't had a chance to talk to Emma again yet because of the level of activity around her bed. And he hadn't even been to check up on how young Mickey was doing.

Neither reason was any excuse to stay in the emergency department, of course, and if they'd been scrambled for another callout Tom would have gone instantly, without a backward glance.

Well, maybe he would have looked over his shoulder but that was perfectly understandable, wasn't it? This rescue had been a major incident. The thought of what could have happened if they'd failed could well come back to haunt him. It was no wonder Tom felt he needed a little more closure than normal.

His partner's curious glance had been slightly disturbing, however. Was Tom already involved on an emotional level? Emma was certainly a very attractive young woman and she had certainly impressed Tom with her courage but it wasn't as though he had any intention of getting more involved with a patient. She had a kid, for goodness' sake, and Tom found them an alien species as far as his social life was concerned. Not only that, she had come to New Zealand to find the kid's father and that hesitation she'd displayed in answering questions about friendship made Tom think that there was a lot more going on than Emma was revealing.

She must have ended the relationship if the

guy still didn't know he had a son but it was pretty obvious things were far from over on Emma's side. Why else would she have come halfway across the world?

Tom shrugged off his reluctance to leave. He picked up the folder of paperwork and nodded at Josh.

'You're absolutely right, mate. It's time to go home.'

'You came back.'

'It was kind of on my way home and I wanted to see how you were doing.'

'Much better.' It wasn't hard to find a smile for Tom but Emma felt strangely shy. He looked very different without his uniform and helmet. Had she really registered what he'd looked like at all in the crisis during which they'd met? It was his voice she had recognised just now when she'd overheard him asking a nurse where she was.

Emma would remember that voice and its capacity to sound reassuring for the rest of her life. She would also remember the wonderful strength of his arms but everything else was a haze. Emma couldn't remember anything after the point they'd escaped the van. She'd looked for Tom when she had woken up enough in the emergency department only to be told that he'd gone and that he'd finished his shift so was unlikely to be back in the department that day. There'd been too much else going on to register disappointment but the pleasure Emma felt now on seeing him come through the curtain of the private area she was now occupying was well up the positive emotional scale.

'Anything still hurting?'

'Not really. Morphine's great stuff, isn't it?'

'What did they find on ultrasound?'

'My spleen's been bleeding a bit but it's not damaged enough to need removing. They reckon it's stopped bleeding now but they want to keep an eye on it for a day or two.'

'And your leg?'

'That's a bit more of a mess. I have to go to Theatre to have it cleaned out properly and stitched.'

'But nothing's broken?'

'No.'

'That's great. You should be up and around in no time.'

'I can't believe I'm going to be up and around at all.' Emma took a deep breath that escaped in a rather shaky sigh. 'You saved my life, Tom. I don't know how to say thanks.'

'You don't have to.'

'All in the line of duty, huh?' Emma caught Tom's gaze and could see perfectly well that her rescue had been something completely out of any normal line of duty. She could also see that he knew she knew that.

For a moment, the atmosphere was heavy as they held the eye contact and acknowledged the significance of what Tom had done.

Emma wasn't sure who smiled first. Maybe her, to try and show Tom how enormously grateful she was.

Or maybe it was Tom. Why would he have come back to the hospital to see her if he didn't want to revel in the satisfaction of an unusually successful mission?

But why did it feel like there was a rather different message being passed with that shared smile?

Emma dropped her gaze, suddenly embarrassed. She was feeling grateful, not *attracted* to the man, for heaven's sake! Never mind that she could still instantly summon the sensation of being held in his arms. He'd been rescuing her, not dancing with her!

'How's Mickey?'

'Hungry.' Emma smiled again, reliving the sheer relief of finding her son had been completely uninjured by the awful accident. And the miracle that she was still alive to care for him. 'They found him a wheelchair and a nice nurse has taken him to the cafeteria with her while she has her meal break.'

'Will they let him stay with you in hospital?'

'They'll have to.' A new and horrible fear reared its head. 'If he has to leave then I'm not staying.' She didn't like the frown on Tom's face. 'You think there'll be a problem with that?'

'I hope not. I know there's never any

question of not letting a mother stay with a sick child. I've just never heard of the reverse happening. Unless it's a breastfeeding infant, of course.' Tom was still looking concerned. 'You're going to need to rest and concentrate on yourself for a little while. Is there nobody that could care for Mickey for you?' He cleared his throat. 'What about his... father?'

'No chance.' Emma turned her face away from Tom, dismissing the suggestion. 'I'll pick my own time to let him know about Mickey, thanks.'

That was something that would have to be handled very carefully.

'Besides, I don't even know if he's available.'

For Mickey or for *her*? Simon had been asking for her in the hospital in London where they'd met. He'd told someone he'd never forgotten her but that didn't necessarily mean he wanted her back in his life, did it? Even if he *wasn't* married any longer. Emma tried to squash the anxiety that had plagued the decision process in planning to come to New

Zealand. She wouldn't want Tom to pick up an undertone and think she was totally desperate. Trailing around the world on the off chance of rekindling a past romance.

'He...travels quite a lot,' she added hastily.

'Right.' Tom sounded disinterested. In fact, he was edging away from her bed. 'Well, I'm glad you're feeling a bit better, Emma. I'll try and get in to see you again, maybe.'

He stepped further away. 'Let me know if there's anything I can do to help.'

His exit route was blocked by the arrival of the emergency department's nurse manager.

'Emma? I'm sorry. I've done my best but there just isn't the bed space to let Mickey stay in with you. We've got someone from Social Welfare coming in to discuss options.'

'What?' Dismay didn't begin to encompass the sinking sensation that hit Emma. *'No!'*

'I'm sorry.' The nurse manager was looking at Tom as he reiterated his apology. Maybe he was looking for some moral support in having to enforce an unpalatable situation. 'I've really done my best.'

'No.' Emma pushed at the covers of her bed. 'I'm not having Mickey taken care of by strangers.'

Luckily, no one had raised the side of her bed. In her drug-induced, pain-free haze, it was remarkably easy to sit up and swing her legs over the side.

'*Emma!*' Tom sounded horrified. 'What do think you're doing?'

'I'm going to find my son.'

'You can't walk on that leg,' the nurse manager declared. 'You'll reopen the wound and start bleeding again. You could start bleeding internally again as well.'

'I really don't care.'

Likewise, Emma didn't care that she was being irrational and probably ridiculous. Her brain was too fuzzy to be able to articulate *why* it would be so unacceptable to have Mickey cared for by strangers, it was far easier to just give in to the overwhelming need to keep her child close by. They'd almost been ripped apart for ever only hours ago. Couldn't these people understand how important it was for them both to stay as close as possible now?

'Emma—please, get back on the bed.' Tom was moving to help the nurse manager.

She pushed his hand away. 'No. I have to find Mickey. Where's the cafeteria?'

The curtain of the area Emma was in was pulled back to admit an orderly. 'All set to go up to Theatre?' he queried cheerfully.

'*No!*' Panic stepped in and brought tears to Emma's eyes. She covered her face with her hands to try and force them back. Getting hysterical was not going to help her win this battle.

'Emma?'

She knew it was Tom's hands holding her arms. Emma knew that touch well. 'What?'

'How 'bout if I hang around and look after Mickey for you? Would you go up to Theatre and get your leg sorted?'

'You can't do that.'

'Why not?'

The nurse manager's voice held the same tone as Emma's had. 'It's not just a babysitting stint,' he said. 'Emma's going to need to be kept in hospital for a few days, mate.'

'So? I've got four days off starting tonight. I can take Mickey home with me.'

Emma swallowed. Hard. She dropped her hands and turned a tear-streaked face up to Tom. 'You'd do *that*?'

'If that's what it takes to make you happy to stay and get the treatment you need.'

'Yes…but…'

'I'm not sure Social Welfare will be all that happy about this, Tom.' The nurse manager was staring at Tom with a very odd expression. 'You're not registered as a foster-parent. You're a single male. You're as much of a stranger as anyone else in Christchurch would be.'

'No.' Emma shook her head vigorously. 'Tom's not a stranger. He saved our lives. Mine *and* Mickey's.'

'But you don't know anything about him.'

'I know enough.'

The nurse manager shook his head. He raised his eyebrows eloquently. 'I suppose they'll make all the checks they feel they need to but, Tom, do you actually know anything about looking after kids?'

'I can look after myself.' Tom sounded puzzled. 'Kids are just short people as far as the necessities of life go, aren't they?'

'This one's a bit special. He'll need extra care.'

Tom's hand was still on Emma's arm. She felt the encouraging squeeze. 'Is he so difficult to look after?'

'Not really.' Emma was happy to respond to the encouragement. She wanted Tom to succeed where she couldn't. It was the only acceptable option given that she wouldn't make it as far as the door if she tried to walk out of here. 'He needs to be carried a lot.'

'No problem.'

'And he still needs to wear a nappy. His bladder control isn't great yet.'

Tom clearly had to rally from a moment of being taken aback. 'I'll manage,' he decided. 'I've got friends with kids. They can give me a few pointers.'

'Mickey can tell you what he needs and how to do it.'

The nurse manager was shaking his head again. 'I don't know about this. It's very irregular.'

The orderly looked pointedly at the clock.

'Either Mickey goes with Tom or I'm discharging myself.' Emma's words came out with admirable firmness. She knew she was going to have to lie flat again in about two seconds. She was feeling sick and dizzy and the pain was biting at her leg again. There was just enough time to smile at Tom. 'Will you bring him in to visit me?'

He had a gorgeous smile. It made his eyes crinkle with genuine warmth.

'You'll probably have to chase us away when you need some rest.'

Emma was still smiling as she lay back against her pillow and let herself sink back into the release of temporary oblivion. Yes, Tom might be a stranger but how could you not trust someone who had risked their life to save you?

He was still saving her.

CHAPTER THREE

FOR the second time that day, someone was suggesting that Tom Gardiner was not thinking straight.

His younger sister, Phoebe, was being even more unkind. She was laughing aloud.

'Oh, man! This is great. What *were* you thinking of, Tom?'

He gritted his teeth. 'I was trying to help someone.'

'By babysitting? Night *and* day? For days and days and—'

'Yeah, I get the message. Stop gloating, Phoebs.'

'But, Tom…' It took a moment for Phoebe to get real control. 'You *hate* kids.'

'I don't *hate* them. I just don't know what to do with them. They make me nervous.'

'So you offer to be *in loco parentis* for an unknown length of time? You're nuts!'

'Look, I thought you might be able to help. I didn't ring up for a dose of sibling abuse.'

But Phoebe giggled again. 'Just wait till Mum hears about this. Oh…that wasn't you we just saw on the news, was it? Dangling over some van that was getting washed out to sea in a river? I told Mum it probably wasn't cos she was having kittens.'

'It *was* me, actually.'

'Holy heck! Just as well you're OK, then. Mum's gone to a lot of trouble making a roast chicken dinner for us. She'd be mad if you didn't show up.'

'I probably won't be able to show up. I'm going to be looking after Mickey, remember?'

'Bring him along. Mum could pretend he's one of those grandchildren she's got her heart set on.'

'I don't think so. He's a tired, frightened four-year-old, Phoebe. He doesn't need another batch of strangers to deal with.'

'Where does he usually live?'

'Wales.'

'Oh…' The penny seemed to be finally dropping. 'Is this something to do with that van in the river?'

'Yeah. I pulled Mickey out before his mother.'

'Is his mother all right?'

'She's injured, but not too badly. She'll be in hospital for a few days and she wasn't keen to have her son handed over to Social Welfare.'

'Hmm.' Phoebe sounded very thoughtful. 'So this mother—she's cute, huh?'

Tom ignored the bait. The batteries on his mobile phone were due to run out any time. 'Phoebe, I've got someone from Social Welfare turning up at the hospital to interview me any second to see if I'm acceptable as a caregiver,' he said crisply. 'I would prefer not to come across as a total idiot.'

'Which you *are,* of course.'

'Probably. Are you going to help me or not?'

'Tempting as it is to see you try and pull this off by yourself, big brother, I'll see what I can do.'

'Thanks.' Tom let his breath out in a huff of relief. 'What do I need?'

'My friend Alice has got kids. Her little boy is three and her daughter's just turned one. She'll know what you need and I'm sure she'll lend me some stuff.' Phoebe laughed again. 'She won't be able to resist if I promise to fill her in on all the gory details later.'

'How soon could you collect stuff?'

'I'll do it now.' Tom could hear a heavy sigh. 'Mum's giving me the evil eye here, Tom. You'd better talk to her. She's not going to be very happy about the meal. What time will you get to your house?'

'I don't know. There's a bit to sort out here first.'

'I won't wait for you then. I'll drop the stuff on your doorstep and then come back here. That way, at least one of us will get to eat dinner.'

'I'll make it up to Mum.'

'You'll have to. How old did you say this kid was?'

'Four. Nearly five but he's very small for his age. He's got spina bifida.'

There was a moment's shocked silence on the other end of the line, which was disconcerting. It was hard to shock Phoebe.

'Tom...? Are you sure you know what you're doing?'

Nearly two hours later, Tom could almost smell the roast chicken dinner he was missing out on. He wished he *had* been able to attend the planned family gathering.

Emma was still in Theatre. The pleasant young woman from Social Welfare had been easily persuaded that Tom was up to the job of caring for a small, slightly disabled boy and had whisked him off to the nearest supermarket to help him purchase disposable nappies and other items deemed necessary.

Tom had collected Mickey from the care of the emergency department nurses to find his young charge was very displeased with the whole arrangement despite having had it explained to him by his mother before she'd been taken into the operating theatre.

'I don't like you,' he reminded Tom, as he was carried to the car park.

'I've got a dog at home,' Tom offered. 'Do you like dogs?'

'No. Dogs bite.'

'My dog doesn't bite.' Tom couldn't think of anything else to offer as an inducement. At least Mickey had been fed and toileted by the nursing staff while Tom had been at the super-market. With a bit of luck, he could just put him to bed once they got home and then have a quiet beer or two while he thought about how to get through tomorrow. He tucked Mickey into the booster car seat the paediatric ward had supplied, along with a small wheelchair.

'It's only for a day or two until Mummy gets better.' Tom was reassuring himself as well as Mickey, he realised. 'It won't be so bad.'

It was bad.

Mickey caught sight of Max—Tom's elderly, long-haired German shepherd—and shrieked with fear.

He refused to be placated with any offers of

food or drink and Tom's delight in finding that Phoebe had left a bag of toys, along with a selection of clothes and even a plate of chicken dinner covered with foil on his doorstep, was rapidly diminished as Mickey hurled one offering after another across the floor of his living room.

Max obligingly picked the rejected toys up and brought them back, one by one, to where Mickey was sitting, howling, on the couch.

'I don't think you're helping, mate,' Tom told his dog sadly. 'Maybe you should go outside for a bit.'

And maybe Tom should ring the appropriate authorities and admit defeat.

But how would he be able to front up and tell Emma he'd done that? What if she woke up in Recovery to learn that he'd betrayed the trust she'd put in him? Tom got a sudden memory of the look in Emma's eyes when he'd taken Mickey from her arms in the van. She had known there was a distinct possibility she wasn't going to make it out of there alive and she had trusted him to take her son to safety and do whatever was needed to keep him safe. The depth of love for her child and the desperate plea for help tugged at something deep within Tom all over again.

There was no way he could betray that trust.

'Do you want to watch TV?' he asked Mickey.

Mickey shook his head and kept howling.

'Do you want to go to bed?'

The small face turned an even darker shade of red and the decibel level increased alarmingly. Small hands punched at Tom so he was forced to move further away. He stood there, looking down at the miserable scrap of humanity on his couch, and felt utterly helpless.

It wasn't a pleasant feeling.

No wonder he'd instinctively avoided having anything to do with kids. In terms of stress levels he'd choose dangling out of a helicopter or climbing into water-filled vehicles any day. Tom had had about as much as he could take.

'I'm just trying to help,' he told Mickey with a sigh. 'But I can't do this by myself, obviously. Do you want me to find someone else to look after you?'

'No-o-o…I want Mummy.'

'I know you do.' So do I, Tom thought desperately. I want Mummy to come and scoop you up and make everything all right.

A thoughtful crease appeared between Tom's eyebrows. The idea was a little embarrassing but who was there to see, other than Max?

'Would a…a cuddle help, buddy?'

By way of answer, Mickey picked up a small, pink dog from the pile on the couch beside him and threw it at Tom. It bounced onto the floor a few feet away.

Max pricked up his ears. He looked at the toy and then he looked at Tom.

'I wouldn't bother.' Tom sighed more heavily this time. 'OK, Mickey. I'm going into the kitchen to get a drink. I'll be back in a minute.'

A beer. Icy cold and refreshing enough to clear his head. Tom popped the tab on the can and took a long swallow. He wondered what price Phoebe might extract from him in order to offer some hands-on assistance. She worked with kids all the time in her job as a physiotherapist. She'd know what to do to stop a kid making himself sick by crying.

He took another swallow. Removing himself from the near vicinity seemed to have helped because the noise level had dropped considerably. It was silent in the adjoining room, in fact.

Tom's beer can hit the bench with enough of a thump to send foam cascading down its side. Had Mickey rolled off the couch and cracked his head on the coffee-table? Was he lying unconscious on the floor while his carer was swigging alcohol in another room?

The panic subsided the moment Tom swung into the living room. He stopped in his tracks as he saw Max nudging the pink dog closer to Mickey from where he must have placed it on the couch cushion earlier.

Mickey was still snuffling and he still looked pretty miserable. He might have been trying to reject Max's offering when he picked the dog up and threw it again but Max was giving him the benefit of any doubt. The dog waved a still magnificent plume of a tail and went to retrieve the toy.

This time there was no mistaking a game had begun. Mickey scrubbed a wet nose with the back of his hand and threw the fluffy pink dog with purpose.

'Go!' he instructed Max.

Max went. So did Tom, slipping back into the kitchen, still unnoticed. Who was he to argue if his dog could do a better job of babysitting than himself? If it was working, Tom was quite prepared to go with the flow.

He took another peep into the living room a minute later. Max, bless him, wasn't even looking bored by the repeated track he was pacing on the living-room carpet. When Tom looked in again, however, Max had given up. He was sitting on the couch beside Mickey.

Normally, Tom would have ordered his pet off the furniture but Mickey had his arm around the big dog. He may not have wanted a cuddle from Tom but accepting the warmth and companionship from Max was something Tom could relate to perfectly well.

Less than a minute or two later, Mickey was sound asleep, his arm still around Max's neck.

When Tom gingerly picked the child up and carried him to the spare bedroom, Max sloped along behind.

Tom agonised over whether he should change Mickey's nappy but decided that it wasn't worth the risk of waking the exhausted child. If he was too uncomfortable, no doubt he would wake and make his needs obvious. Tom would cope when he had to but why invite a new crisis when this amazing peace had settled in his disrupted household?

Max seemed to agree. He lay down beside the bed and put his nose on his paws with a heartfelt sigh. Tom drew the duvet up to cover Mickey's arms and then paused, caught by the sight of the sleeping child.

It was hard to believe he'd been so upset a short time ago. There was no sign of any misery on the small features now. Dark eye-lashes sat like butterfly wings on pale cheeks and there was almost a hint of a smile on the soft-looking pink lips.

Emma's lips had that same soft look to them. Tom had to shake his head a little to stop himself wondering what Mickey's mother might look like when *she* was asleep.

The thought that she might not be asleep right now sent Tom to the telephone. He wanted to ring and reassure her that everything was all right. Emma *was* awake, apparently. Still drowsy after her surgery but a lot more comfortable. The nurse who relayed Tom's message had a smile in her voice when she returned to the phone.

'She said to say thank you. And to tell you that you're a hero.'

The echo of the smile that message had given Tom only really vanished the next morning when he went to Mickey's room to find Max stretched full length on the narrow bed with the small boy's arms wrapped firmly around his neck. A shaggy tail gave an almost imperceptible and very apologetic wag but Max made no move to get his paws on the floor where they belonged.

The thought of what the authorities responsible for ensuring the proper care of defenceless young children would have to say about it was a bit of a worry.

'I don't think we should tell Mummy that Max slept on your bed,' Tom said as he got Mickey up.

'Why not?' Mickey really was an expert in looking suspicious.

'Well, some people don't think dogs are all that clean. And that they should sleep in a kennel outside or at least on the floor.'

'He was keeping me warm.' The tone suggested that Tom would be confirming a lack of trustworthiness if he tried to stop Max sleeping on Mickey's bed in the future. 'I *like* Max,' Mickey added firmly.

The look was eloquent. Mickey may as well have had a balloon over his head saying, "And I don't like you, remember?' Tom had to suppress a grin. He was starting to understand what made this kid tick. He had a lot of his mother's courage. He was prepared to fight to protect a new friendship he had chosen but he wasn't ready to let Tom invade the space he shared with Emma.

Being changed and washed by Tom that morning was an ordeal for both of them but the incentive of going to visit Emma straight after breakfast saw them through the rather fumbled necessities.

And the smile on Emma's face made it all worthwhile.

Emma had a lot of pillows on her bed. Several were behind her back, allowing her to sit up comfortably, and more were keeping her leg raised. Some minor adjustments were necessary to make space for Mickey to sit beside her and Emma prudently put one pillow between herself and her son.

'Try not to sit on my tummy, darling. It's still a wee bit sore.'

Mickey nodded, his face shining, his whole body tense with the effort of sitting still waiting for his mother's hug. He was attached like a limpet virtually the instant Emma held out her arm and she pressed more than one kiss to the curls on the top of his head.

'Are you being a good boy for Tom?'

Mickey's voice was muffled against Emma's neck. 'I'm *always* good.'

'Hmm.' Emma raised her gaze swiftly enough to catch the tail end of a somewhat contradictory look on Tom's face. She smiled, trying to convey her gratitude for all Tom was doing for them both.

Mickey didn't seem too traumatised by his first real separation from her. The initial hug had been fierce but he was relaxed and happy in her arms already. Maybe he'd made things difficult but Tom was clearly coping.

He looked away from her, as though the gratitude she hoped she was radiating was embarrassing. The toes protruding from the heavy bandaging on her leg seemed to be of great interest to Tom.

'Your skin colour looks good,' he commented. 'Not too much in the way of vascular damage, then?'

'Apparently nothing they couldn't repair. I believe there are a lot of internal stitches and a pretty massive scar on the outside.' Emma's tried to make light of the injury.

'Just as well I wasn't planning any beauty contests for a while.'

Tom glanced up and it was Emma's turn to feel embarrassed at the message she received. She hadn't been fishing for compliments. Looking away even more hurriedly than Tom had a few seconds ago, Emma focused on Mickey.

'That's a cool T-shirt you're wearing, hon.'

Mickey nodded, pulling back to stare down at the picture on the front of the garment. 'It's Power Rangers.'

It was also not Mickey's shirt, which was disconcerting. Emma had to catch Tom's eye again. 'You haven't been spending your money on clothes for Mickey, I hope?'

Tom shook his head. 'My sister has a friend with a son who's about the same age. She arranged a loan.'

'That's so kind of her!'

Tom's grin was wry. 'I'm not sure the motive was entirely altruistic. Phoebe's expecting me to fall in a huge heap, trying to look after Mickey. I suspect she wants enough input to feel justified in gloating.'

'I hope there's been nothing to gloat over so far.'

'No.' Was that a forced brightness in Tom's tone? 'We're having fun, aren't we, Mickey?'

'I like Max,' Mickey told his mother.

'Who's Max?' For a moment, Emma felt a shaft of disappointment. Maxine, perhaps? Tom's *wife*?

'Max is my dog,' Tom said.

'Oh.' That surge of relief was entirely inappropriate for more reasons than one. Emma squashed it ruthlessly. What had she been thinking of? Mickey was terrified of dogs. 'Um…what sort of dog is Max?'

'A German shepherd,' Tom said.

'A *clever* dog,' Mickey said at the same time. 'He can play with me.'

Relief had definitely been out of order. Emma loved dogs herself but she had a healthy respect for a breed like German shepherds. Her anxiety must have shown because Tom was smiling at her.

That same gorgeous smile that had yesterday brightened the most terrifying ordeal of her life. It seemed bigger today. *Tom* seemed bigger. His presence was almost overpowering in the confines of the private side room of the ward Emma was in. She might have expected him to be less physically impressive out of his paramedic uniform, especially dressed so casually in faded, blue denim jeans and a soft-looking, open-necked white shirt, but the opposite was true.

And that smile! That 'trust me, everything's going to be just fine' smile.

As if Emma didn't trust him already. Tom had risked his own life to save Mickey. He was hardly likely to endanger a small boy by letting him play with a dangerous animal, was he?

Emma smiled back. Until she realised she had been holding eye contact with Tom just a shade too long. She looked away hurriedly.

'I'll have to thank your sister. I lay awake last night worrying about things like clothes. I don't suppose there's any chance of recover-ing any of our stuff from the van, is there?'

Tom was shaking his head. 'Not possible,

sorry. I checked with the police this morning. Most of the small stuff was washed out to sea and divers couldn't see anything they thought was worth retrieving. It could be a few days before they drag the van out of where it is now but I wouldn't get your hopes up.'

'Oh…' Emma cuddled Mickey close again. 'That's not good. All our clothes. Our passports. Mickey's wheelchair…and his callipers.' Emma's intake of breath was a gulp. 'Just when he was starting to walk so well with them.' The threat of tears loomed as Emma contemplated their situation. So far from family and friends. She couldn't ask Tom for any more help—he was already doing far more than he probably wanted to.

Tom was smiling at her again. Maybe he didn't need to be asked. He had to be the *nicest* person Emma had ever had the good fortune to meet.

'We'll get it sorted, don't worry. The paediatric ward can do without one of its wheelchairs for a few days and we've got plenty of clothes. Have you got travel insurance?'

'Yes, but all the papers were in the van.'

'Can you remember the company you used?'

'Yes, I think so.'

'Leave it with me, then. Mickey and I will go and let you get some rest. I'll look into the insurance stuff before we come back this afternoon.'

Tom shrugged off Emma's thanks with the same nonchalance with which he had just shouldered her current burdens. She watched him leave with her son and felt no qualms about Mickey's eagerness to get back to his new friend Max.

They seemed to be taking her stress with them and Emma could feel herself smiling as she lay back on her pillows and let a period of healing sleep claim her body again.

'I don't *believe* it!'

'You talking to me?' Phoebe's gaze was still riveted to the television screen where yet another cartoon on the satellite channel was under way.

'Not really.' Tom dropped the phone onto the couch cushion beside him and raked his fingers through his hair in a gesture of frustration. 'I've just talked to what must be the sixteenth person at that insurance company. It's already taken two days and I don't think I'm any further ahead.'

'At least you've found a real person to talk to instead of the automated answering service.'

'At this rate it'll be Christmas before Emma sees any money. She's due to be discharged tomorrow and she can hardly leave wearing that hospital gown, can she?'

'I can lend her some clothes. What size is she?'

'How would I know something like that?'

'Hey, Mickey?' Phoebe propped herself up on her elbows and turned to her companion, who was still transfixed by the animated action on the television. 'Is your mum fat?'

Mickey nodded.

'Really?'

Max thumped his tail in appreciation of Phoebe's fascinated tone but leaned closer to Mickey, who had one hand buried in the shaggy fur of the dog's neck.

'She is not fat,' Tom declared. He could remember very clearly just how slim that body had been. How easy it had been to hold her as they'd been winched to safety in the helicopter. 'She's as skinny as you are, Phoebs.'

'How tall is she?'

'I don't know.' Tom hadn't seen Emma standing up yet. 'Not short, though. Probably about your height.'

'How old is she?'

'Twenty-eight.' Tom remembered that much from filling in the patient report form.

'Gosh, she was quite young when she had Mickey, then.'

'I guess.'

'Very young.' Phoebe sat up and swivelled to face her brother. 'Accidental, huh?'

'Shh.' Tom frowned a warning for Phoebe to try and curb her tendency to cut straight to the chase. Mickey was clearly not listening to the adult conversation but Phoebe took the hint anyway.

'How long is she going to stay?'

'Until the insurance gets sorted. They can't go anywhere until the temporary passports get here. Which reminds me…' Tom reached for the telephone again. 'I've got another call or three to make.'

'And I'd better get going. I've wasted half my day off already.' Phoebe got to her feet.

'Not wasted,' Tom assured her. 'You've been a great help. You're good with kids.'

'I should be—it's my job.' Phoebe ruffled Mickey's hair. 'See you later, kiddo.'

Mickey just nodded again. Max would have accompanied Phoebe to the door but Mickey still had a death grip on his fur. His tail waved an apology.

'I'll drop in tomorrow,' Phoebe announced as she passed the couch. 'I'd like to meet Emma.'

The assumption was startling. 'What makes you think she's coming here?'

Phoebe easily outdid Tom in sounding surprised. 'Where else has she got to go?'

Where else indeed? Without even a means to identify herself, let alone a credit card, Emma might find it very difficult to get accommodation at a hotel or motel.

Besides, Mickey's mother was still recuperating. She couldn't be expected to cope all by herself. But Tom only had one more day off before he had to go back to work.

Life was getting more complicated by the minute.

Phoebe was watching Tom open and close his mouth and she grinned happily at her brother's obvious dismay.

'You didn't really think you were going to get your empty and boring house back to yourself so soon, did you?'

'It's not boring. Or empty.' Tom looked towards Max and his eyes widened. 'Good grief!'

Phoebe followed his gaze and her grin widened. 'Cool. Good boy, Max.'

'Should he be doing that?'

Phoebe shrugged. 'Why not? If Max wants to be a walking frame it's his call. Looks like good physio to me.'

It looked alarming to Tom. Max was standing up and must have pulled Mickey to his feet. The dog seemed oblivious to the discomfort of having large tufts of his fur providing an anchor for a child who was far from steady on his feet. If Max tried to move, Mickey would fall flat on his face and it would be Tom that would have to try and pick up the pieces.

He frowned at Max.

Max waved his tail. Very gently. And that was the only muscle the dog was moving.

'I'll drop some clothes around later,' Phoebe said. 'You can feed me if you like.'

'Thanks. What would you like for dinner? Barbecue OK?'

'Don't mind.' Phoebe paused at the door. 'Hey, Mickey? What's your favourite thing to eat?'

'Fish and chips.' Mickey was still standing beside Max. A huge smile had replaced a look of intense concentration. 'Look at me, Phoebe!'

'I'm looking. That's awesome standing but don't do it for too long at a time, will you? Your legs will get very tired.'

Mickey was sitting on the floor again by the time Tom closed the door Phoebe had left open. He was laughing aloud at the cartoon.

Tom picked up the phone but didn't dial a

number. Somehow the urgency of sorting out Emma's logistical hassles had diminished.

Why hadn't he pre-empted Phoebe's assumption that Emma would come to stay for a few days? It was perfectly logical. Why upset Mickey with another move in a strange city when he was quite happy where he was, thanks largely to Max and now Phoebe? And he himself would be around at least part of the time, which would mean Emma could still get some of the rest she was going to need.

Another peal of laughter from Mickey was contagious enough to make Tom smile. Maybe his sister had hit the nail on the head. Even with Max around the house *was* going to feel pretty empty when Mickey was gone.

Reuniting Emma with her son and having them both there in his home for a few days wasn't just logical.

It simply felt…*right*.

CHAPTER FOUR

'ARE you sure about this, Tom?'

'Absolutely.'

'I love your house.'

'It's just an old villa that needs heaps of work done but there's plenty of space.'

'I'll say. It's huge!'

'Four bedrooms. Two of them are a bit full of junk, though, so I've put you in with Mickey, if that's OK.'

'Perfect. I've missed him so much.' Emma leaned on her crutches for a moment, waiting while Tom lifted her son from the car seat in the back.

'Max!' Mickey shouted happily.

Something that looked remarkably like a wolf bounded around from the back of the house. Emma's jaw dropped. *This* was Mickey's new best friend?

The dog appeared to be grinning and it was showing every one of an impressive set of huge white teeth. Mickey should have been scared silly but he was laughing aloud, stretching down from Tom's hold with both arms. Tom bent down far enough for Mickey to grab two bunches of fur and amazingly the dog stood completely still, apart from waving his tail.

Emma cleared her throat. 'He…um…looks friendly.'

She got the full blast of *that* smile and something inside Emma melted. Tom knew exactly how alarmed she was by the reality of Max and while he might think it was unjustified, he wasn't about to dismiss her fear. He was happy to reassure her instead. And to offer trustworthiness.

And Emma was more than happy to accept.

'It won't be for long,' she assured Tom as he showed her through his comfortable house. 'I'll be back on my feet properly in a few days and then I'll get us sorted.'

'When's the follow-up appointment at the hospital?'

'Four days from now. Hopefully, by then, the insurance will have come through. And then…' Emma paused, having nodded her appreciation of the bathroom facilities she was seeing. What *was* going to happen then?

Tom looked curious as well. 'Yes?'

'And then I'll be ready to contact Simon.'

'Simon?'

'Mickey's father.'

'Oh.' Tom's tone suggested complete disinterest. He turned abruptly and Emma followed. This was a little disturbing. Was Tom bothered by her plan to contact Simon? Why? Maybe it was an echo of that disapproval she had sensed during her rescue. That she had raised a child alone for nearly five years and had never given the father the right to know about, let alone have anything to do with, his own son.

Did it strike a chord that was more than theoretical? Did Tom have a child he wasn't allowed to be a father to? Somehow that notion was more disturbing than being disapproved of and there was evidence that it might not just be her imagination. There seemed to be a lot of toys in the house. A trail of them led from the hallway back into the living room where Mickey was…

'Oh, my God!' Emma gasped.

Mickey was standing beside the wolf, tufts of black tipped fur protruding from tight little fists. About to move very swiftly to rescue her son, Emma found Tom's hand on her arm.

'He's OK,' Tom murmured. 'Watch.'

Emma watched, her mouth dry and her heart beating a tattoo on her ribs. She could feel every one of Tom's fingers burning an impression through her clothing and into her skin.

She had thought the dog was standing still but he seemed to lean forward now. As Mickey lurched, Max took a very careful step and by some miracle, Mickey was still upright… having taken a *step*.

'He just did that last night for the first time,' Tom whispered. His mouth had to be very close to Emma's ear because she could feel his words as clearly as she could hear them and a shiver ran down her spine. 'I think he's pretty proud of himself.'

The smile on Mickey's face as he looked up to see his audience was more than proof of that. Emma felt tears sting her eyes. With not a calliper or walking frame in sight, her little boy was on his feet.

Briefly. With a plop, Mickey sat down. He was still grinning as Max wiped a long tongue up his cheek and Emma wasn't going to say a thing about germs.

'Did you see me, Mummy? Did you see me and Max?'

'Mmm.' Emma had a lump in her throat that made it hard to get any real words out.

'Phoebe reckons it's good physio,' Tom said. 'Until we can get something sorted at the department.'

'Phoebe? Your sister?' Emma looked down at the jeans and sweatshirt that that were only a size or so too loose. 'The one who's been kind enough to lend me everything?'

'Yeah.' Tom smiled proudly. 'Did I mention she's a physiotherapist?'

'No.'

'A very good one. She works with kids like Mickey all the time. She's been visiting a lot so if you're around long enough to want some treatment for him, she can sort it and Mickey won't feel like he's having to deal with a whole lot of strangers.'

'Phoebe likes fish and chips,' Mickey informed his mother. 'And cartoons.'

Emma had to sit down. To catch her breath.

To chase away this curious—and disturbing—sensation that she was *home*.

That she had stepped into a fairy-tale ending for this chapter of her life.

That what she was feeling for Tom Gardiner at this moment was an awful lot more than gratitude for the help and friendship he was offering so generously.

It was a hard call. Emma must have swayed slightly on her feet, which would explain why Tom's hand was on her arm again, guiding her towards a wonderfully comfortable-looking sofa.

She shouldn't be feeling the imprint of his

hand like this, however. So much stronger than moments ago. A tingling sensation that went straight to a place deep in her abdomen.

Emma lay back on the couch and closed her eyes with a sigh. She was exhausted, that was all. Suffering a lack of physical strength that was making her overly sensitive to someone showing her kindness. It was all too easy for a woman to mistake that for something more significant.

She opened her eyes to see Mickey doing his curious bottom shuffle to move across the floor. She helped him onto the couch and cuddled him, burying her face in his sweet-smelling curls.

Her precious son was safe, that was what really mattered here, and the love Emma felt for her child was enough to remind her that it was wrong to continue hiding his existence from his father. She didn't need Tom's unspoken disapproval to push that message home.

Mickey deserved all the love he could get in his life and he deserved to have a father. As soon as Emma felt strong enough, she would do whatever was necessary to bring them together.

And that fantasy of her reunion with Simon?

Strangely, that seemed to hold far less appeal than it used to.

'Target sighted, nine o'clock.'

'Roger. Turning downwind.'

The move to double-check his harness fastening was automatic. Tom's brain was busy registering a sensation of relief as the next and far more dangerous phase of this callout began.

The relief wasn't due to any tension from having difficulty in locating their target. The group of climbers on New Zealand's highest mountain were experienced and had been able to give a specific location to the plateau they were on.

'Secure aft.' Josh craned his neck as he peered from the window of the helicopter. Impressively sheer rockfaces slid past beneath them, the deep snow filling crevasses blindingly white. 'Checking winch power,' he added.

Tom drew in a deep breath. The relief wasn't due to knowing that getting to the climber in trouble was time-critical either. The man was in severe respiratory distress, possibly due to a heart attack or high-altitude pulmonary oedema, which could prove easily fatal without a rapid descent and aggressive oxygen therapy. That kind of tension never undermined Tom's state of mind during working hours.

'Turning base leg.' Terry, the pilot, sounded completely focused. 'Three hundred metres to run.'

Within seconds Tom would be on the move. Following a protocol that was automatic but could never be taken lightly. And that was where the relief was stemming from. From now on, this job would require every ounce of Tom's concentration and energy. He let out the deep breath he had been unconsciously holding and allowed himself another moment of relief.

For a while, at least, there would be no room in his head for thoughts about Emma.

'Speed back. Clear door,' Terry instructed.

The helicopter slowed and then rocked a little as Josh slid the door open.

'Door back and locked,' he told Terry. 'Bringing hook inboard.'

Tom attached the hook to his harness and checked the fastenings. He unclipped his safety belt and watched Josh for the signal that he was ready.

Josh gave a terse nod. 'Moving Tom to door. Clear skids.'

'Clear skids.' Terry was ready to make adjustments for the extra weight on one side of the helicopter as Tom was winched out.

Seconds later, he was dangling below the skids. Looking down over the lightweight stretcher attached to his harness, Tom could see the faces of the people below as they watched the rescue unfolding.

One of the climbers was a young woman. Tom could see strands of dark hair whipping around the white helmet she wore in the blast of air from the helicopter rotors.

And, for a split second, Tom thought of Emma again.

The way her long, dark hair swung and rippled over her shoulders when she moved. The almost uncontrollable urge that had been building for days—of wanting to bury his fingers in those tresses. To use that soft, dark cloud as an anchor to draw Emma's face close to his. Close enough to touch her lips with his own.

The flash was gone as quickly as it had appeared. There were no thoughts of Emma as Tom's feet touched the rough rock of the plateau and he unhooked himself from the winch line.

'Quick!' someone shouted. 'I think he's just stopped breathing.'

'What's his name?'

'Dave.'

'Has he been conscious until now?'

'Yes. He was talking to us when you were on the way down.'

Tom crouched beside the climber. 'Dave— can you hear me?' He rubbed his knuckles on the man's sternum, trying to elicit a response to a painful stimulus. There was no response. Tom could see the dried frothy sputum on his patient's face. He could also see the blue tinge of cyanosis on his lips that was more than could be expected from the cold temperature of the environment.

'He seemed fine,' the young woman said brokenly. 'A bit of a headache and a cough but that was all. He *said* he was fine.'

Tom could feel a pulse in Dave's neck. It was rapid and weak but it meant that the information he'd received so far was accurate. The respiratory arrest could have only happened moments ago because continued hypoxia would have resulted in cardiac arrest within a very short period of time.

There was still a chance of saving the climber. Tom needed to evacuate this patient as soon as possible and get him to a lower altitude. Had he still been breathing Tom would have put him straight on the stretcher and waited until they were safely on board the helicopter to start any treatment, but that wasn't an option now.

'I'm going to have to intubate Dave and get as much oxygen as possible into his lungs before we move him,' he told the climbers. 'Could someone take his helmet off, please?'

Stripping off his outer gloves, Tom swiftly pulled equipment from his pack. A laryngoscope, endotracheal tube, connection apparatus and lubricant.

'Anything else you can tell me?' Tom queried. 'Does Dave have any medical conditions? Did he have a fall?'

He had attached the tiny portable oxygen cylinder to a bag-mask unit as he spoke. Squeezing the bag forced air into Dave's lungs.

'He looked drunk,' a man said. 'He couldn't co-ordinate himself on that last stretch.'

'He slipped,' the girl added.

She sounded frightened. Tom gave her a brief smile. 'Could you hold Dave's head for me, please? In this position.' He tilted the unconscious man's head and placed the girl's hands on either side. She would benefit by being involved here. It was possible that Dave's fall while roped to the other climbers had been a narrow miss for a much larger disaster. This young woman still had to negotiate the rest of their descent and thinking too much about what had nearly gone wrong would make it a dangerous ordeal.

'He doesn't have any medical conditions,' she told Tom. 'He was fitter than any of us.'

Tom peered under the blade of the laryngoscope, trying to visualise the epiglottis. Had it been a heart attack? The onset was sudden for high-altitude pulmonary oedema. It could have been crippling chest pain that had caused the clumsiness. Or had Dave been making light of earlier symptoms such as a headache and shortness of breath because he was determined to finish the climb? Maybe even to impress this dark-haired girl who was holding his head steady.

Not that it mattered.

Tom could see the vocal cords as he lifted the blade of the laryngoscope. He slid the tube into place and connected the oxygen supply, watching the chest-wall movement as he squeezed air in under pressure.

A few seconds with a stethoscope to confirm

equal air entry and then a few more to tie the tube securely into place, but the entire procedure had taken less than a minute.

'Right. I'll need some help to get Dave onto the stretcher.'

His helpers were willing and capable but the frigid air temperature was biting at Tom's fingers by the time he slid the buckles of the straps into place to secure Dave to the stretcher. He took just a little more time to squeeze more oxygen into his patient before the enforced break the winching would entail.

A signal to Josh once he had secured the winch hook to both the stretcher and himself meant that he was about to leave the other climbers.

'Is everyone else OK? Are you going to need any help getting down?'

'We're OK,' the girl said. 'But what about Dave? Is…is he going to make it?'

'He's very sick,' Tom told them honestly, 'but we'll do everything we can.'

He could hear Josh talking to Terry over the radio, warning the pilot that the weight was coming onto the winch line. And then he was dangling in mid-air again, steadying the stretcher as they spiralled slowly on the way up to the helicopter.

'Is he going to make it?'

The wide, dark eyes could have belonged to Dave's climbing companion but this time the wish for a successful outcome was showing on Emma's face.

'He was looking a hell of a lot better by the time we left the emergency department.' Tom picked up his fork again with a sigh of pleasure. 'This is delicious.'

'It's only shepherd's pie.'

'You didn't have to cook for me.'

'I wanted to.' Emma turned to the wheel-chair parked beside her at the end of the kitchen table. 'Don't play with your food, Mickey. Use your fork, not your fingers.'

She seemed to have abandoned for own meal for the moment in favour of quizzing Tom about the afternoon's mountain rescue.

'It must have been so exciting.'

'It was a good job. I had my doubts about

whether we'd even get him to hospital alive when I found he wasn't breathing.'

'Did he regain consciousness?'

Tom nodded, his mouth full.

'What will they do for him now?'

Tom swallowed. 'Probably not much more than we were doing, apart from some drug therapy. They've started him on a calcium channel blocker.'

'Why?'

'It lowers the raised pulmonary artery pressure and helps clear alveolar oedema, which improves oxygenation.'

Emma nodded her understanding. Tom had to avert his gaze when she began eating again. How on earth could watching someone eat shepherd's pie be so astonishingly sexy?

Distraction was at hand with the change of view.

'We don't feed Max at the table,' Tom reminded Mickey. 'He's got his own dish in the laundry, remember?'

'Mickey!' Emma's chair scraped on the floor. She limped a step towards the bench and scooped up a damp cloth to wipe the remnants of pie from her son's hands. Max wiped crumbs off his nose with his tongue and Mickey giggled.

'I want to do that,' he announced.

'What?' Tom was grinning. 'Wipe your nose with your tongue?'

'Yes.'

Emma gave the tiny nose a playful swipe with the cloth. 'I don't think so.'

Mickey giggled again as he made a grab for the cloth, which Emma whisked from reach. Tom's grin widened. It was such a delicious sound, this little boy's laughter—kind of like the gurgle of pipes that were in dire need of a plumber's attention. Tom had been hearing it with increasing frequency in the days since Emma had come home with him and it never failed to make him smile.

Did Emma's laugh sound anything like that? Tom hadn't heard it yet, which wasn't so surprising, but she was looking far less tired and sore now. She was smiling a lot more but not laughing aloud.

Tom wanted to make her laugh. Not just to hear whether the sound was as contagiously joyful as Mickey's laugh but because he wanted to be able to make her feel that good.

He wanted to make her that happy.

When Emma glanced up as she sat down again, her face stilled and Tom realised that something had surprised her. Then she smiled. *At him.* It seemed a lot harder than normal to take his next breath.

He could almost believe that Emma really liked him. *More* than really liked him. That her warmth was not simply gratitude for being helped out of the dire predicament of being injured and alone and penniless in a foreign country with a disabled child to care for.

Tom's appetite deserted him and the silence suddenly became awkward. It was Emma who broke it hurriedly.

'I heard from the insurance company today. The cheque's in the mail, apparently.'

'That's great.' Or was it? Would Emma use the money to buy tickets to return home? It had only been four days since her release from hospital, though. She wasn't really well enough yet to travel such a long distance. Or was she? 'Hey, how did your appointment at the hospital go today?'

'I can start weight bearing properly on my leg.' Emma smiled brightly. 'And the rest of me is fine.'

Tom's nod was more agreement than satisfaction. The rest of Emma was a lot more than fine in his opinion.

'I went down to the emergency department to thank everyone for looking after me and especially for the way they looked after Mickey—and guess what?'

'What?'

'I got offered a job.'

'Really?' A thread of excitement caught Tom. The thought of Emma staying for while and working at the hospital where he would see her often was vastly preferable to the image of waving her goodbye at the airport.

'They're really short-staffed. Screaming out for nurses. I could do whatever shifts fitted in with looking after Mickey. They gave me a list of child-care centres that some of the staff use. One of them even caters for children with special needs.'

Tom tried to keep his tone casual. 'Would you be interested?'

Emma opened her mouth to respond but then closed it abruptly. She twisted in her chair.

'Mickey? Have you had enough to eat?'

'Yes.'

'Want to go and play with Max for a bit before your bath?'

'Can Max have a bath with me?'

'No.' Emma stood up and lifted Mickey from his chair. 'But he can come and watch.'

They were both silent as they watched Mickey shuffle across the floor. With surprising speed he vanished through the door, with Max close behind. Tom waited for Emma to speak because her expression suggested that she had something she hadn't wanted to say in front of Mickey. Sure enough, she waited only until the plume of Max's tail disappeared.

'I'm not sure what I should do, Tom.'

'Tell me.'

Emma hesitated. She avoided meeting Tom's gaze. 'I told you that one of the reasons I came here was to contact Mickey's father?'

'Yes.' The reminder was a splash of cold water. A wake-up call. 'Have you found him, then?'

Emma shook her head. 'He works at the hospital. The nurses in ED wanted to look after Mickey while I had my appointment with the surgeon and so I took a few extra minutes to find his office.'

Tom was confused. 'Who's office? Did you get lost?'

'No. Simon's office.' Emma cleared her throat. 'Mickey's dad is a neurosurgeon. He specialises in spinal work.'

'In Christchurch?' A redundant question but Tom was buying a little time. The cold feeling from that wake-up call was intensifying. Mickey's father had to be an attractive prospect. Intelligent. Well respected. Probably extremely wealthy.

'Not right now.' Emma's brief smile was wry. 'He left town yesterday on a lecture tour to the States and UK. He won't be back till the end of the month.'

'That's more than three weeks away.'

Emma nodded. 'That's what I'm wondering about. Do I stay and wait for him to come back or should I take Mickey home?'

Stay, Tom wanted to advise. I don't want you to leave. But did he want her to stay because she was waiting for a reunion with another man? What would Emma think if she knew how uneasy that made him feel?

It was easier to say nothing but the silence felt even more awkward this time.

'It seems crazy to have come all this way and then go home without even talking to him,' Emma continued. She was still avoiding eye contact with Tom. 'And I couldn't just tell him he has a son and then disappear again, could I? He might want the chance to get to know Mickey.'

Tom's nod was slow. Of course Simon would want to get to know Mickey. No doubt he'd be more than keen to get to know Emma again as well.

Emma sighed. 'But it's a long time. I couldn't afford to stay…unless I *did* take that job at the hospital.'

'Would your visa allow you to work?'

'I didn't need a visa to come here. As a British citizen, I can visit for up to six months without one. It sounds like it wouldn't be a hassle to get a temporary work permit so I *could* stay.'

Six months was a long time. A lot could happen over a period of time like that.

'And I'd have to find somewhere for us to live.'

'You could stay here.' The words were out before Tom could consider the repercussions.

'For six months?' Emma's jaw dropped. 'I couldn't do that!'

'Why not?' Tom could have answered his own question perfectly easily. Because if the way he felt about Emma grew even a little more he could be setting himself up for a personal disaster of unprecedented proportions. But his brain was refusing to co-operate with the warning signals. Words that could only spell trouble kept emerging. 'This house is huge. Mickey's happy here.' Tom kept his tone light. 'Hey, *Max* is happy. It's nice heading off to work, knowing that he has some company for a change.'

Emma's eyes were huge. And shining. She believed him. 'I'd pay rent, Tom. I can do that if I take that job.'

'Do you want to? Take the job, I mean. I wouldn't want you to pay rent.'

'Of course I'll pay. You've done so much for us already.'

'That's what friends are for.'

'And I would *love* to work in Emergency again—even for a little while. It was my favourite place in the hospital. Just listening to you talking about your work in the last few days has made me realise how much I miss it.'

'So you'll stay?'

Emma nodded. 'If you're really sure, Tom.'

Tom wasn't sure of anything except that he didn't want this woman to disappear from his life. Not just yet, anyway. So he nodded.

'I'm sure.'

'Then I guess we'll stay for a bit, anyway. We can see how it goes.'

As Emma finished speaking, Max appeared in the doorway with the pink soft toy dog dangling in a very undignified manner from his teeth. Large brown eyes suggested that a break from babysitting duties would be welcome and Emma laughed.

And it *was* the same delicious gurgle that Mickey had.

As Emma limped from the kitchen to find her son, Tom realised, just a little too late maybe, that he was lost.

Was this what falling in love felt like?

If he looked back in years to come, would he pinpoint that moment when Emma had laughed as the one in which his life had irrevocably changed?

Warning bells sounded too loudly to be ignored now. Emma's a no-go area, Tom reminded himself sternly as he cleared the table. She's just admitted that she came halfway round the world to find the man who was the father of her child. If she'd only wanted to inform him, she could have written a letter.

And falling in love shouldn't feel like this, he decided as he washed the dishes. So bitter-sweet.

It could simply be a case of extreme physical attraction, in which case it shouldn't be too hard to take a step back. He'd *have* to take a very large step back if the attraction was one-sided anyway.

What the hell had he been thinking—to invite Emma to stay for another month or more?

Sliding the last plate into place on top of the stack in the cupboard, Tom knew what he needed to do in order to find safer ground. The opportunity came a short time later when Emma returned from getting Mickey into bed. She saw the extra mug of coffee on the table.

'Is that for me? Thanks, Tom—you're an angel.' She sat down. 'This is *exactly* what I need.'

And Tom knew exactly what he needed. He nodded and then spoke decisively.

'Tell me about Simon,' he commanded Emma.

CHAPTER FIVE

THE question was startling.

Emma had been rather reluctant to mention Simon at all after her initial impressions of Tom's disapproval, and when she had disclosed her dilemma of whether or not to stay in New Zealand to await Simon's return, there had been that odd little silence. Did Tom really want to talk about her ex-lover? Why? And why did Emma really not want to? Because there were so many other things she loved to talk to Tom about? Or was there a deeper reason she was avoiding? Such as her growing feelings for this man?

'Um...' Emma looked down at her coffee-mug. 'What would you like to know?'

'How did you meet him?'

That seemed safe enough to talk about. 'He

was on sabbatical and he had operating privileges in the London hospital I worked in. He was invited to demonstrate the techniques he specialised in and I happened to be the scrub nurse in Theatre that day.'

'And he was impressive?'

'Oh, yes.' Emma couldn't help sounding convincing. Simon had been a very impressive man. No more impressive than Tom was in his own field, but Simon had the glamour and charisma of a very successful surgeon and she had been a young and impressionable nurse. 'The field of laparoscopic spinal surgery was very new back then. It was astonishing stuff. Simon noticed I was interested and invited me to attend some of his lectures.'

'Hmm.' Tom sounded as though it was just what he had expected to hear. 'So he was around for a while?'

'No. Only for a couple of months. He was spending part of his time in the States.' Emma hoped that Tom wouldn't ask how long it had been before the relationship had started because it seemed far too quick in hindsight.

A matter of days. About as long as she'd known Tom, in fact, but Emma had always known very quickly whether she found a man attractive.

Tom was so very different to Simon.

But no less attractive.

'How did you find out he was married?'

Emma snorted. 'His wife turned up. She said she had come to London for a spot of shopping and needed his credit card. Funnily enough, I was waiting for him at the time myself. I was planning to tell him I was pregnant.'

'What did you do?'

'I showed his wife a chair she could sit in and then I walked out. I resigned the next day— told them I had a family emergency and wouldn't be able to work out any notice. They were very good about it.' Emma's smile was poignant. 'I guess I was convincing because it was kind of the truth.'

'And you haven't spoken to him since?'

Emma shook her head.

'You must have been very upset.'

'Yes.' A small word. It couldn't begin to encompass the devastation Emma had experienced.

Tom's voice was very quiet. 'You must have been very much in love with him.'

'Of course I was.' Emma looked up but ignored what looked like sympathy in Tom's eyes. 'I don't sleep with someone I'm not in love with, Tom.'

He looked away. Emma could see a muscle twitching in his jaw and it seemed like Tom was coming to terms with something he didn't like. Or maybe he was letting go of the prejudice he'd been holding against her. For a second Emma stared at his profile. He had a strong face, this man. Almost rugged. You'd never guess the kindness he was capable of. Unless you saw that smile. There was no hint of that smile on Tom's face as he turned back to her. Emma had never seen him look this serious.

'Are you still in love with Simon, Emma?'

Emma drew in a deep breath. What if she said no? If she confessed that it was getting harder by the day to even remember what Simon looked like?

There had been moments—ever since she had first seen Tom during the nightmare of her rescue—that Emma had thought Tom might be attracted to her, but what if she was wrong? He already seemed to have reservations about the way she'd handled the moral issue of Mickey's father and whether he should have been told about his baby. What would Tom think if she admitted she had come to find Simon but now felt attracted to someone else? Not much, probably.

If nothing else, after all he'd done for her and Mickey, Emma owed Tom her honesty.

'I thought I was,' she admitted quietly. 'For a very long time I felt betrayed and angry but after last year I wasn't so sure.'

'What happened to change things?'

'Simon went to London. He went to find me at the hospital where we'd met.'

'He went all the way to London to find you?'

'It sounded like it. I heard through a friend who'd heard from someone else. It sounded like Simon was now separated from his wife and had come to try and find me.'

'Did no one tell him where you were?'

Emma shrugged. 'The story was a little garbled by the time I heard it. Someone my friend knew had been in the pub with a group of theatre staff and it had just been an item of gossip. I didn't pay that much attention to it at first but then I started thinking that maybe I'd been wrong.'

'Not telling him about Mickey?'

'Yes. And maybe by walking out on him like that. If he's divorced now, maybe the marriage hadn't been very happy in the first place. That might have been why he didn't think I needed to know about it.'

'Hmm.' Clearly, Tom didn't agree. He gave his head a small shake as though he wanted to change the subject. And he did.

'Were your parents supportive?' he asked.

'Very. They did their best and it was a wonderful start. Especially when Mickey was born and we found out that he wasn't quite perfect. I don't think I could have coped very well with that on my own. Everybody was supportive, really. It's just a quiet little village but it has its advantages and it's not very far from the kind of medical treatment and schooling that Mickey needs.'

'So you'll go back there?'

'I don't know.' Emma sighed and picked up her coffee, which was cooling rapidly. 'I set out on this trip with grand ideas about starting a whole new life that was more exciting than the old one.'

'You couldn't have got off to a more exciting start, that's for sure.'

'Mmm.' Emma didn't want to go there again. The accident haunted her enough as it was. 'It wasn't a very good omen, was it? Maybe I'm not supposed to find Simon.'

Or maybe she had been supposed to meet Tom. Life had a funny way of turning corners rather abruptly sometimes.

Tom was giving her a strange look. 'Are you having doubts that you want to find him?'

Emma's heart picked up speed. There was no mistaking the undertone in the look she was receiving.

'I…I'm not so sure any more.'

'Why not?'

'I feel confused,' Emma admitted. 'I'm not sure how I feel about Simon any more because…'

'Because you know that I'm very attracted to you?' Tom asked quietly.

Emma's mouth was dry. 'No. It's because I…feel the same way about you.'

Oh, *God*! Why on earth had she confessed *that*?

She stared at Tom with something like horror. His hand moved as though he was about to take Emma's. Then it stopped.

'This is complicated, isn't it?'

Emma had to nod.

'It's not a path either of us should be going down until things are less complicated.'

Emma thought of Mickey tucked up and hopefully asleep down the hallway. He'd had enough trauma in the last week without making life any more difficult for the moment. She nodded again.

'You won't really know what you want to do until you've had the chance to talk to Simon again, will you?'

'I guess not.' Emma wished she could deny her confusion. She could see that Tom wasn't happy. 'I'm sorry, Tom. This changes things, doesn't it?'

'What things?'

'You won't want me living here.'

'Why not?' Tom looked thoughtful. 'I think it'll actually be a lot easier now that I know I'm not imagining some one-sided attraction here. We don't have to act on it.'

'No.' Strange how disappointing it could be to be doing the right thing.

'The important person in all this is Mickey.'

'You mean he needs his father?'

'Not necessarily. But his happiness really depends on his mother's happiness. You're going to have to do what's right for you.' Tom stood up. 'And I'm not going to complicate that any further for you.'

'You're sure you're OK with us staying here?'

'Yes.' Tom smiled at Emma. A real smile. 'We're friends, aren't we?'

'Absolutely.'

'That's not going to change. No matter what else happens.'

He must have been mad.

Had he really believed that knowing the attraction was mutual would make things easier?

That knowledge had created a whole new dimension to every moment of his time with Emma. Even the moments he wasn't with her. It was a little easier at work because the knowledge stayed quietly in the background. An occasional thought that could be pleasurable, like knowing there would be a hot meal and good company waiting when he got home or a little anxious thought, like wondering how Mickey was going in the physiotherapy session Phoebe had organized, or whether he liked the specialist day care centre the first time he went and whether Emma was coping with her first shift in the emergency department. Thinking about them didn't interfere with how well he did his job, it just seemed to add colour to his life.

At home, it was a different story. Everything

had taken on a new significance. Every conversation. Every moment of eye contact. Every accidental or unavoidable touch, like when Emma passed him a cup of coffee or Tom picked Mickey up and then transferred him to his mother's arms. At home, the knowledge was like a living entity—hungry to feed its own growth with any morsels, even as small as a direct look or a peal of laughter.

The day Phoebe had taken Emma shopping after her insurance payment had come through had been a moment of truth. She had purchased jeans and a soft sweater that went perfectly with denim, pale, cream wool clinging to parts of her body that Tom had not realised were quite so stunning. Yes… Just being in the same room with Emma now was enough to feed his growing feelings and knowing that it wasn't one-sided seemed to have granted licence for fantasy. Private moments when he thought about what could be.

Something else was growing at the same time, however. Something far less pleasant. At first it was just part of the knowledge. Simon was Mickey's father. Emma would be doing the right thing in finding him and telling him about his son. Both Simon and Mickey had rights here that couldn't be ignored. So did Emma. She had to find out what she wanted. What was best for *her.*

Tom had no illusions that things could be a lot worse for him than living with the frustration of unexplored attraction. It was quite possible, given their living arrangements, that the spark between himself and Emma could be fanned into the beginnings of a real relationship, but Tom wasn't about to start something that could be killed in its infancy.

It would be unfair on everybody involved if Emma discovered she was still in love with Simon and the surgeon was willing to make them into a family. He himself would suffer a hell of a lot more than he did at present. Simon could well be adversely influenced if he knew that Emma had been seeing someone else while awaiting his return. He might reject Emma and his son, and where would that leave any of them?

A lot less than happy, that's what. And more than anything Tom wanted Emma to be happy. He didn't seem to be able to control moments of fantasy that included Emma rejecting Simon and wanting to be with him more than anybody else in the world but, for the moment, the realm of fantasy was where they had to stay.

Until the job that came nearly two weeks after that revealing conversation with Emma. When life had settled into a remarkably pleasant routine and Emma was loving her part-time work at the hospital and Mickey's balance was improving enough for Phoebe to present him with a pint-sized pair of crutches to try.

Any job that meant the transfer of a patient to Emergency at a time when Emma was on duty was welcome so initially it was a disappointment to be rerouted on their return from the nasty accident on an isolated stretch of mountain road. The driver of the van had a serious spinal injury and the SERT crew was instructed to deliver him directly to the specialist spinal unit on the outskirts of the city.

Tom had not been to Coronation Hospital for a long time and the opportunity it represented might not have occurred to him if he hadn't spotted someone he knew in the team of medical staff waiting on the outskirts of the helipad to meet them. Megan was a nurse he had dated briefly a few years ago and they had parted very amicably when she'd set out for an overseas adventure. Not that he had time to give more than nod a greeting at first. Handing over their patient was the first priority and the medical director of the unit was among the waiting team.

'This is Bruce Robinson,' Tom told him. 'Forty-six years old. High-speed MVA and he was carrying timber in the back of his van. A fairly hefty beam went through the back of his seat and he has a crush injury between about C6 and T2.'

The doctor leading the team nodded briskly as he walked behind the stretcher beside Tom. The information had already been relayed by radio but the walk into the hospital was the ideal time to review the case so far.

'When we arrived he already had significant paresis and paraesthesia,' Tom continued. 'GCS was 15 but breathing was diaphragmatic, BP was 90 on 50 and he was bradycardic at a rate of 54.'

It became quieter as they got further away from the helicopter, whose rotors were still slowing, and the doctor moved to intercept the stretcher as it passed through the doors of the spinal hospital.

'Hi, Bruce,' he said. 'I'm Patrick Miller. We're going to check you over carefully and see if we can find out exactly what the damage is and the best way to treat it. How are you feeling at the moment?'

'Cold,' the man said miserably. His face was pinched by the collar protecting his neck and his forehead covered by the straps securing his head to the backboard. 'I can't move my legs and I've got pins and needles in both hands.'

Patrick put a sympathetic hand on his patient's shoulder. 'How's the pain?'

'Pretty bad.'

'We'll do something about that in a minute.'

Tom filled the doctor in on the drugs they had administered so far as they sped towards the assessment area. His use of morphine had been judicious due to the potential respiratory complications in a patient with a high spinal injury.

The procession slowed a little as they rounded a corner. Megan was holding a nearly depleted bag of IV fluid aloft and Josh had to steady the portable oxygen cylinder hanging from the head end of the stretcher. Tom put the brakes on and fell behind just a little as Bruce was wheeled through another set of double doors.

That was when he saw the gallery of photographs on the corridor wall. Mugshots of the consultants that cared for the patients admitted to this specialist hospital. Patrick Miller's was first, of course, and there was a surprising number of others, but Tom couldn't resist keeping his pace slow enough to scan the names at the bottom of the pictures.

And there he was. Simon Flinders. Neurosurgeon.

The impression only lasted a split second before Tom let the double doors swing shut and cut it from view but it stayed in his mind with astonishing clarity as he waited in the assessment area. It would be a while before he and Josh could return to the helicopter. Unless there was an urgent summons, Bruce would not be moved from their stretcher and backboard until all the initial examinations and X-rays had been completed and he and his partner could well be needed to assist with logrolling Bruce during the first procedures.

There were a few minutes of nothing to do, however, as the first X-rays were taken and pain relief topped up for Bruce. Tom found himself unable to shift that photograph from his mind. Even as a male, he had to admit that Simon Flinders was exceptionally good-looking with abundant, wavy, sun-streaked hair and a charming, boyish grin.

That picture must stand out for anybody walking down that corridor because Simon was the only member of the elite medical staff who didn't look suitably serious. With a smile like that, he was probably as popular with the staff as he was with patients and their families—especially if he was as good at his job as Emma believed. No wonder she had fallen for him.

Presumably, Mr Flinders spent a significant portion of his working time at this hospital. Tom assumed he would have a private practice as well and he had to spend a lot of time at the main city hospital to have an office there, but the staff at Coronation Hospital would probably know him as well as anyone. And the staff here included someone Tom considered to be a friend. Megan would know about Simon, even if she hadn't had much personal contact with him.

She looked as though she'd be more than happy to talk to him later. Her smile was warm as she dusted Tom's forearms and hands with talcum powder in preparation for logrolling Bruce.

'I'll be doing the counter-bracing,' Megan said. 'Tom, can you put yourself in the middle and take care of the abdominal section?'

'Sure.' Tom slid one arm under Bruce's thighs and placed his other arm across the top of his body to hold his waist.

'On the count of three,' a registrar instructed from where he held the head steady. 'One, two…three.'

Bruce was turned carefully and his spine was examined thoroughly. When the logroll was reversed, a full neurological examination was carried out and Tom couldn't help wondering if Simon Flinders was as good at what he did as Patrick Miller.

Probably better.

Tom's usual level of interest in watching the examination was tainted and his mind wandered as the discussion among the medical team became focused. Results were being collated and decisions made regarding surgery and the initiation of the high-dose methylprednisolol regime that could minimise ongoing damage to Bruce's spinal cord. The authority and skill of the senior staff was palpable. So was the desperation from their patient that something could be done to save him being paralysed for the rest of his life.

Someone capable of this level of medical care had to be far more impressive than a paramedic. Especially someone with the physical and probably financial assets a particular consultant surgeon was blessed with.

When the helicopter's gear was finally able to be collected, Tom was pleased to see Megan staying behind to help clear the assessment area.

'How are you, Megan?' Tom curled up the electrode wires from the life pack and tucked them into a side pocket of the carry case. 'I haven't seen you for years.'

'I'm great. And you?'

'Never better.' Which was perfectly true in some ways, Tom decided. Life felt completely different since Emma and Mickey had appeared. More important. More colourful. 'How was your time overseas?'

'Fabulous. I got married.'

'Wow! Good for you. Who's the lucky guy?' Tom was perfectly sincere but was also aware that he had no pang of regret for missing his opportunity with a woman he had liked very much. There was only one woman who held any interest for him now.

'His name's Bill. I met him in Scotland where he was driving a tour bus.'

'How long have you been back?'

'Over a year now.'

'You like working here?'

'Love it. I got really interested in working with spinal patients while I was in Scotland.'

'Hmm.' Tom nodded encouragingly. He took the oxygen cylinder from Josh and laid it on top of the mattress stretcher. 'I've been hearing a bit about the advances in laparoscopic surgery lately. You've got someone that specialises in it here, haven't you?'

'Simon Flinders? Yes. He's brilliant.'

'So I've heard.' It was a bit harder to sound casual now. 'Nice guy?'

'Depends who you're talking to.' Megan chuckled. 'The patients adore him.' She gave Tom a curious glance. ' Why do you ask?'

'I know someone who knows him. Or knew him, anyway.'

'Ah.' Megan's tone carried a wealth of under-standing. 'Don't tell me—she's a nurse, right?'

The impression Tom was getting was not one he liked. 'So he's a bit of player?'

Megan grinned, cast a glance over her shoulder and then lowered her voice. 'He's not called Simon Fingers just because of his name or surgical skill.' Then she shrugged. 'Not that it's a problem for me. Or his patients.'

It was a problem for Tom, though. A reputa-tion entrenched enough to give someone a sleazy nickname was a shock. It was not good enough for someone like Emma. Or for Mickey. This wasn't about personal jealousy. Tom's protective instincts had been roused from the first moment he'd caught a glimpse of Mickey and his mother.

The feeling that they might still need his pro-tection was sharp enough to seem urgent.

By the time Tom had finished his conversa-tion with Megan he was seriously concerned. Did Emma have any idea of what Simon was really like? If she was prepared to excuse him not mentioning the fact he had a wife, it was possible she would dismiss the kind of information Tom had just been made privy to. He wasn't about to say anything but he tucked the new knowledge away. Maybe the competition had just tipped a fraction in his favour.

Emma changed from her uniform into her jeans and sweater as soon as she arrived home. Maybe she'd see that gleam in Tom's eyes again tonight—like the way he'd looked at her the first time she had worn her new clothes.

Not that she should be encouraging any attraction he felt for her. How unfair was that when she'd confessed to coming to this country in order to chase up an ex-lover? It was selfish to revel in the confidence that knowing she was still desirable fostered.

But it was equally compelling.

As compelling as it was to spend time with Tom. To talk to him and share every detail of her new life.

'Work was so good today. Really busy but I didn't get too tired. I'm not even limping much.'

'Anything interesting?'

'Mostly routine. I had someone in a diabetic coma and a teenage drug overdose that was a bit messy. You must have had a quiet day.'

'Why's that?'

'You didn't come into Emergency.' Emma kept her tone light. It wouldn't help anything for Tom to know that part of the enjoyment of her new job was seeing him arrive in the department with a new patient. A big part.

'We had a major extrication from an MVA in the mountains. The driver had spinal injuries so we took him directly to Coronation Hospital.'

'Oh.' Emma looked away from Tom in the hope of finding a new topic of conversation that would seem natural. Did he know that Simon worked at Coronation Hospital? The sight of Mickey playing with Max was perfect inspiration.

'Phoebe says that it's Max who's responsible for Mickey's balance getting so good. She reckons they could employ him in the physiotherapy department.'

'I think he prefers an exclusive clientele.'

Tom was grinning as he got up to answer the phone and had to avoid his dog taking measured steps across the living room floor with Mickey half riding on his shaggy back.

He had the telephone in his hand when he returned. 'It's your mum,' he told Emma. 'Want me to start Mickey's bath?'

'That would be fantastic.' Emma took the phone. 'Mickey, do you want to say hello to Grandma before you go and have your bath?'

'Grandma!' Mickey shouted into the phone seconds later. 'I can *walk*!'

Emma had to temper her mother's excitement after Mickey had been carried away to the bathroom.

'He's only standing, really. The crutches are a bit much to manage but Phoebe says we can look into having some new callipers made if we're going to be here long enough.'

'So you're not thinking of coming home yet?'

'Not yet, Mum.'

I *am* home, Emma thought suddenly as a childish giggle, followed by loud splashing sounds, wafted into the room from the direction of the bathroom. If only things weren't quite so complicated. If…

'Sorry, Mum, I didn't hear that.'

'I was asking about this job of yours. Are you sure you're not trying to do too much? It's only been a few weeks since that dreadful accident. Your dad wants to talk to you about your leg.'

It took a while to reassure both her parents that she was fine, and by the time Emma finished the call, the house was very quiet.

She found Mickey tucked up in bed, with Tom reading him a story, and the sight of her son's sleepy, contented face made that feeling of being home so intense it was almost painful.

Bending down to kiss her son, Emma had to avoid looking at Tom. The urge to kiss *him* was potentially overwhelming.

'Grandma says I can have a dog when we go home,' Mickey said.

'Did she?' Emma had even more reason not to catch Tom's gaze now. It wouldn't be fair to let him see how disturbing she found the idea of having to leave.

Mickey was unaware of any undercurrent. 'When *are* we going home, Mummy?'

'Don't you like it here, sweetheart?'

'Yes.' Mickey's eyes were half-shut and he snuggled more deeply into his pillow. 'But we came to find my daddy and we've found him so don't we have to go home now?'

Emma sank onto the side of Mickey's bed, only dimly aware of how wobbly her legs had become. She had no hope of avoiding looking at Tom now and he was clearly as shocked as she was.

'What makes you think we came here to find your daddy, Mickey?'

'I heard Grandma talking to you before we came on the aeroplane.'

Emma closed her eyes for a moment. She'd had no idea any such conversation had been overheard. She had to lick very dry lips before she could speak again.

'And...and what makes you think we've found him?'

'Cos Tom reads me stories. That's what daddies do.'

Tom had his eyes closed now. Emma focused on Mickey. It was ridiculously hard to find the words but she had a duty she had no choice not to perform. She had to be honest.

'Tom isn't your daddy, darling.'

Big brown eyes, so like her own, were suddenly visible again.

'Why not?'

Emma could feel her lips twist into a sad kind of smile. What a good question. If Mickey had a list of qualities he might want to find in a father, she had no doubt that Tom would make the grade despite Mickey's initial antipathy. Would she have to go through that suspicion and reluctance to share her attention with Simon? And would the resulting relationship have any chance of being such a success?

'Because I hadn't met Tom when you came along,' she told Mickey carefully. Would Tom pick up the unspoken message that if she *had* met him first, things would be very different? Emma didn't dare risk another glance to find out. She had something else to say and now seemed as good a time as any.

'Your daddy's name is Simon,' she told Mickey.

'Where is he?'

'He's been away for a while but he's coming back soon.'

'When?'

It was difficult to swallow. Emma stared at the corner of Mickey's duvet, which had somehow become entangled in her fingers. When she spoke, her voice sounded unnaturally high. Forced. As though the word was an unwelcome guest but had to be admitted.

'Soon.'

Too soon, in fact.

Simon was due back in Christchurch the next day.

CHAPTER SIX

IT WAS all too easy to postpone what had to be done.

Turning up, unannounced, in Simon's office was probably not the best plan, Emma decided. Maybe she should drop a note into the internal mail system in the hospital to give him some warning.

Or maybe she should wait a few days to make sure he wasn't jet-lagged and totally unreceptive.

Maybe she didn't actually want to see him at all, which might pre-empt the ending of this chapter of her life she was sharing with Tom and Max and Phoebe.

Especially Tom.

He had been strangely quiet since the night Mickey had shocked them both by revealing his understanding of Emma's hidden agenda for the adventure of coming all the way to New Zealand. Not that Tom had said anything. On a couple of occasions it had been on the tip of Emma's tongue to ask how he'd felt at Mickey's assumption he was his father. Had he been horrified? Was there a faint possibility that he might *like* the idea?

The question remained unasked, however, because Tom had noticeably stepped back. Direct eye contact was much less frequent and accidental touch carefully avoided. Tom seemed to be spending longer hours at work and he'd gone to his mother's for dinner last night. Mickey appeared to have forgotten the conversation about Simon and made no further queries about his 'real' father, but it was obvious to Emma that Tom was waiting to hear how the meeting had gone.

Emma had nothing to tell him. The tension was getting destructive but she was feeling an increasing sense of panic about doing anything to resolve it. Two days had gone past. Then three. And four. It was so easy to find excuses. She wasn't at the hospital every day. She'd had a very busy shift with too many sick people to look after and she was tired. Mickey had a sniffly nose and she didn't want to leave him at the day-care centre any longer than she had to. Grocery shopping needed to be done because it was her turn to cook dinner. Goodness knew how long she might have left things if the situation had not been taken abruptly from her control.

If she hadn't, quite literally, bumped into Simon Flinders in the hospital staff car park.

It was Emma's fault. Her mind was elsewhere as she negotiated the parking area on her way to the bus stop. One of her patients that afternoon had been a seven-year-old girl with a life-threatening asthma attack. The terrified child had required aggressive treatment and had ended up being intubated and admitted to the intensive care unit. Emma was focused on the comfort she had given the girl's mother, hoping that the reassurance she had given so freely had not been misplaced. It was what she would want herself if it was Mickey that was in such a precarious state of health, wasn't it? Some hope to cling to? Reality would intrude fast enough if things became worse. Or should she have been brutally honest and told the mother there was a definite possibility that her child would not survive?

It was the bleep of a car's remote locking system being activated that made Emma look up and become aware of the imminent collision but it was way too late to avoid it. The man crossing her path was watching his vehicle—a sleek black BMW a short distance ahead—as he pressed the remote. He was a lot taller and heavier than Emma and her balance still wasn't perfect anyway. She was lucky the exposed spare wheel on the back of an SUV was there to meet her outstretched hand and break what could have been a nasty fall.

'You're bloody lucky it wasn't a car that just hit you,' Emma was informed in no uncertain terms. The tone was exasperated, as though the owner of the voice was in a hurry to get somewhere else and didn't appreciate a delay. 'Are you all right?'

'Yes.' Emma had recognised Simon already.

A split-second impression as she had been knocked sideways that had been confirmed the instant he'd spoken.

She straightened slowly, trying to buy enough time to collect herself. Her heart was hammering. Was this sensation of shock due to the surprisingly hard impact of colliding with another pedestrian or was she now feeling so shaky and flustered because she was seeing Simon again?

The man she had once loved and then hated with equally powerful intensity.

Emma turned to face him.

'I wasn't looking where I was going,' she said. 'Sorry.'

Her last word hung in the air as Simon stared at her. Emma had the crazy thought that it could seem like an apology for something quite different.

Like walking out on their relationship.

Or not telling him he had a son.

She couldn't look away. It was too important, for some reason, to try and gauge Simon's reaction when the stunning moment of recognition had worn off. Would she see the truth? That he *had* loved her as much as he'd claimed or that she'd been just a holiday fling and that a reappearance in his life would be the last thing he wanted?

If her presence was unwelcome she wouldn't have to tell him about Mickey, she thought wildly. That way, she could protect her child from any evidence of rejection.

But Mickey knew that his father was here somewhere. Emma would still have to explain why there wasn't going to be any kind of meeting. Why on earth had she felt the need to be so honest with her son? To tell him his father's name?

Her confusion escalated as she stared back at Simon. He hadn't changed much. A few more grey hairs couldn't prevent her being transported back in time to when she'd been a naïve young nurse only too willing to be swept off her feet by a tall, charismatic and impossibly good-looking older man.

'Oh, my God!' Simon said softly. *'Emma!'*

Analysing what she could see in Simon's

expression was tricky. There was astonishment, of course. That was only to be
expected. But there was a lot more as well.
Amazement, perhaps. A hint that Simon had
taken the same backward steps in time that
Emma just had.

Yes. There was much more than simply recognition there and it made Emma feel awkward.

'Hi, Simon,' she said into the new silence.
'How are you?'

Simon just shook his head, as though trying
to clear it. He turned and walked a couple of
steps and then turned back.

'I don't *believe* this,' he exclaimed. *'Emma!'*

Emma was grateful for the continued support
of the spare wheel beside her. She leaned on it,
oblivious to whatever grime the tyre cover could
be leaving on her pale blue uniform. She wasn't
quite so oblivious to how much time was
passing and that she was highly likely to miss
her bus but Mickey couldn't tell the time yet and
the day-care centre would be open for hours.

This was certainly not a situation she could
walk away from. Fate had decided to end her

procrastination and there was a sensation of relief at knowing the waiting was over.

Simon had stopped walking. He was standing even closer now—beside where he'd dropped his briefcase at the moment of impact—but he made no move to stoop and pick it up. He was staring again.

'But what are you doing here?' A gaze that could probably be described as hungry swept down Emma's body and then back to her face. 'You're in uniform!'

'I'm working in ED.'

'Why?'

'I'm a nurse, Simon, remember? I... needed a job.'

'But why *here*? And how long have you been here?'

'Not long. I've only been working for a couple of weeks. And it's only part time.' The questioning was disconcerting. Emma couldn't decide whether Simon was appalled or pleasantly surprised to find her on his home territory.

'What made you choose Christchurch?'

'I…um…it's a long story.'

'You knew I lived here, didn't you?'

Words deserted Emma. This was moving too fast all of a sudden and she felt totally out of control of both the speed and the direction of this conversation. She needed time to get her head together. To try and sort out the conflicting emotions aroused by seeing this man again.

Simon read her silence rather too accurately. 'Did you want to see me again, Emma?' The start of a satisfied smile tugged at one corner of his mouth. 'Is that why you came here?'

He was more than confident the answer would be affirmative. The faint smile only echoed the spark of interest Emma could see in his eyes. She hadn't been able to help watching the movement of his lips. How many memories did she have of what those lips were capable of? The way she'd felt the first time Simon had kissed her? The way his smile and his confidence had obliterated any reservations she had held regarding the tumultuous start of their affair?

'You look fabulous,' Simon told her. 'You haven't changed at all.'

But she had changed. Simon's smile wasn't having anything like the effect on her it had once had. There was no reciprocal stirring of physical attraction as Simon's gaze fastened on her own lips. None at all.

Emma had grown up in the last five years. She was older and wiser. She was a mother.

Simon seemed to sense a lack of appreciation for the compliment he had bestowed. The beginnings of his smile vanished and deep lines appeared at the corners of his eyes as his expression hardened. The stare Emma was subjected to was now painfully intense.

'Why did you do it, Emma?'

He wasn't talking about her arrival in Christchurch any longer. It was typical of Simon's style to cut right to the chase. To get what he wanted out of any interaction with other people.

'Why did you walk out on me?'

'You know why.'

'No, I don't.'

Somebody walked past them and gave the couple a curious glance. Simon nodded curtly and then looked over his shoulder. Was he hoping they weren't being observed by too many other people?

And that only served to remind Emma of the misery of discovering she had been nothing more than a mistress. Something to be hidden discreetly away from public view. To be picked up and played with only when it had suited Simon. In her naïvety she had believed that discretion had been necessary because she had been merely a junior nurse and Simon Flinders a visiting and well-respected consultant surgeon. The misery of discovering the truth had morphed into an anger that was very easy to tap into again.

'I met your wife, Simon.' Emma was pleased at how strong she suddenly sounded. Her knees had finally stopped shaking and there was no echo of any wobble in her voice. 'The one you hadn't bothered to tell me about. Of course I walked out.'

Simon looked away but Emma had the

distinct impression that he was irritated rather than discomfited. Then he shrugged. There was no hint of apology to be seen in his face when he turned back to Emma.

'I tried to look you up when I was in London again last year.'

He hadn't tried to find her when she'd walked out on him, though, had he?

'I hadn't forgotten you,' Simon added. And now he was really smiling. Showing those perfect white teeth and exuding the kind of charm that had been his most attractive feature. 'Damn, it's good to see you again, Emma.'

She wasn't going to be sucked in by that smile. Or the palpable charm. Simon had just dismissed the trauma their past relationship had caused her with a shrug.

A *shrug*! Any suffering Emma had endured was of no importance. The well-remembered charm had been switched on like a light. It was calculated and shallow. Just like that smile.

Nothing like a smile from Tom, which could be nothing less than genuine.

Would Emma be judging Simon like this if she didn't have Tom to compare him to? Probably not. Maybe she could have convinced herself that the change of demeanour and the sudden pleasure of her company gave credence to any one of a dozen reunion fantasies she had conjured up in the last year or so.

But Tom was there. Almost like a physical presence standing close to her. She could imagine his expression—one that agreed wholeheartedly that Simon wasn't the man she had fantasised about. That any warmth was purely superficial. But that he still had the right to know he had a son.

'I hadn't forgotten you either, Simon.'

It was now or never, Emma decided. She may as well get the worst of this interview over with. A car backing out of a nearby parking slot reminded her of how public the place was, but what did that matter? Emma had no desire to go anywhere more private with Simon. Not when his gaze currently suggested he was more than happy to shrug off any bygones and rekindle their acquaintanceship.

Emma took a deep breath. 'It was a little hard to forget you when I was busy raising your son.'

Simon blinked, which apparently activated the off-switch for the charm. And the smile.

'I beg your pardon?'

'I said that I was raising your son.' It was easy to find the words she needed now. 'We weren't all that careful, if you remember, Simon, during our little fling.'

Simon's jaw visible slackened. 'Was that all it was for you, Emma? A *fling*?'

Of course it hadn't been but Emma wasn't about to admit it. She raised her chin. 'Funnily enough, I had been on my way to tell you I was pregnant the day I met your wife.'

'And you *kept* the baby?' The underlying astonishment in his words created a whole new emotion for Emma.

Relief.

Thank goodness she hadn't found Simon that day. How much pressure would she have been subjected to to terminate an unplanned and unwelcome pregnancy? She might have been in love enough to allow herself to be persuaded that it would be in everybody's best interests to make it go away.

Her precious son might never have existed.

Emma simply stared at Simon by way of a response and he had the grace to flush uncomfortably.

'Of course you did,' he muttered. 'Good for you.'

'I should apologise for not informing you at the time,' Emma said calmly. 'I realise I was withholding knowledge that you had a moral right to have.' It seemed a good time to give Simon a taste of his own medicine and shrug off the importance of her actions. 'To be honest, I didn't think you deserved the truth when you'd been less than honest with me.'

'So why tell me now?' Simon shut his eyes and seemed to be concentrating on drawing in some fresh oxygen. 'I've got a family already, Emma. My youngest is only eleven.' He scratched the back of his head. 'Do you need money? Is that why you've come now?'

'I'm not here to ask you for money, Simon.'

'So why *are* you here?'

'I felt guilty that you had a child you didn't know about. That Mickey had a father he was never going to meet.'

'Mickey?'

'Michael. Michael James White. He'll be five in November.'

Simon frowned. Maybe mental calculations were not a favoured occupation. 'And you're sure he's mine?'

That did it. Emma straightened and turned away.

'Wait!' Simon laid a hand on her arm. 'I'm sorry. That was a crass thing to suggest.'

Emma could feel the pressure from his hand. The last time Simon had touched her it would have sparked instant desire.

The way Tom's touch could now.

Simon's hand felt like a dead weight. The touch of a stranger. Emma yanked her arm free.

'We need to talk about this.' Simon pushed a wrist clear of his pinstriped suit jacket and looked at his watch. 'Right now, though, I'm getting seriously late for the first appointment at my private clinic.'

'Don't let me hold you up,' Emma said dryly.

'How long are you here for?'

'I don't know,' Emma responded. 'That rather depends.'

'On what?'

'On whether you have any interest in getting to know your son, I suppose.'

Simon took a step back. He held up a hand. 'Hang on, here, Emma. I need some time to think about this.'

'Oh?'

'Of course I do. Be reasonable. You've had more than five years to get used to this. I've had all of five minutes.' His breath came out in an incredulous huff. 'I'm in the middle of a rather messy divorce. There's issues relating to the children. I really can't afford to have any more flies appearing in the ointment. This isn't particularly good timing, I'm afraid.'

Emma actually laughed but there was no amusement in the sound. 'It wasn't particularly good timing for me when I had our baby, Simon. I coped.'

'I'll cope, too,' Simon snapped. 'But I need time and I need your assurance that this matter will remain strictly between us.' His tone softened. 'I just need a little time, Emma. I need to talk to my solicitor. There's a lot riding on the outcome of the court case my ex-wife is insisting on. Whether or not I can take the job I've been offered in the States depends on it. If it goes my way, I'll be in a much better position to do whatever I need to do to help you and…and the boy.'

The implied help was financial. Emma's gaze flicked from Simon's expensively tailored suit and Rolex watch to the sleek, latest-model BMW his remote had unlocked. Simon had a privileged life where money was no object. Was that something that Mickey deserved to have available? The best kind of therapy and aids and education for a child with his disadvantages did not always come cheaply.

And what if something happened to her?

Mickey's grandparents were the only family he had and they weren't getting any younger. A stepfather, however willing, could never be expected to take on the kind of responsibility a blood relative would be morally obliged to. Did Emma have the right to forgo that kind of back-up on Mickey's behalf?

'Maybe we could meet in town, say, next week?' Simon was taking her silence as acquiescence. 'I know, I could take you out to dinner. Somewhere nice.'

It always had to be somewhere 'nice' for Simon. He wouldn't be content to eat in a kitchen with a large dog and a sometimes noisy small boy.

Simon's tone softened to a silky drawl. 'I'd like that, Emma. I think you might enjoy that as well.'

His touch may not have sparked a physical reaction but that particular tone of voice stirred something not unpleasant in Emma. Simon still found her attractive. He still wanted her.

The reaction was so fleeting she knew it was

simply a memory but it implied that something could be rekindled if she wanted it to be.

Did she want that?

Should she want it? For Mickey's sake?

'Just us, Emma,' Simon whispered. 'Somewhere a bit more private.'

'Just us.' 'Somewhere private.' Where had Emma heard those particular phrases spoken in the very same seductive tone? A very persuasive tone.

This was the man who had just shrugged off the emotional repercussions Emma had suffered from being so easily persuaded once before. And this time Emma wasn't tempted. Not one little bit. The worry that pushing Simon away could be detrimental to Mickey had to be ignored for the moment. In any case, 'just us' seemed to resonate with a new significance. Mickey was a complication Simon didn't want to address. Was her child simply going to be shrugged off as well?

'No,' Emma said firmly. ' I don't think that would be a good idea, Simon.'

'Oh?' Simon didn't like being rejected. Steel

was showing beneath the silk again. 'Fair enough. I'll get in touch with you when I'm ready to talk about this, then.' He picked up his briefcase. 'Just remember that this stays private.'

'And if it doesn't?' Emma was curious to see what Simon might reveal if pushed a little. She didn't bargain for the flash of fury in his eyes.

'I'll make sure you regret it,' he promised.

The threat was clear. Emma shouldn't allow it to frighten her but a chill ran down her spine despite her resolve. What could Simon do? It wouldn't matter if he ruined her job prospects by having a quiet word with fellow consultants. Emma could always go home.

But that would mean leaving Christchurch. Leaving Tom.

And what if he could start some kind of custody battle over Mickey, just to punish her?

The risk was there, however slight. Simon must have seen a flash of fear in Emma's face because he nodded as he turned to leave.

And Emma just stood there, watching until

the black BMW picked up speed as it left the car park.

The driver of that car wasn't the man of any fantasy. Emma was no longer in love with Simon Flinders, that was for sure.

She didn't even *like* him!

Something was wrong.

Tom could sense that the moment he walked in the door that evening.

He was late. A job that had taken his team upcountry to a logging accident in a remote forest had been prolonged and difficult. And unsuccessful. The unfortunate man who'd been in the way of a tree coming down in the wrong direction had suffered crush injuries beyond anything Tom and Josh had been able to deal with.

The aftermath of the tragedy could have been enough to explain why Tom had taken his time to get away from work. The informal debrief of talking it through with colleagues while they cleaned and replaced gear was usually the best way to deal with jobs like that.

It wasn't the entire explanation, however. Tom had been spending noticeably more time at work in the last few days when there had been no difficult jobs.

He might not want to admit it, even to himself, but Tom was dreading the day he arrived home to learn that Emma had had her meeting with Mickey's father. That the surgeon was overjoyed to find her back in his life and that Emma and Mickey were going to be whisked away to make a family that would completely exclude him.

It looked as though today was the day.

Emma wouldn't look at him. She was totally focused on Mickey, who had just finished his dinner and was being herded towards the bathroom when Tom arrived home.

'There's dinner in the oven for you,' Emma called over her shoulder. 'I'm just going to get Mickey into bed.'

Perfectly normal words. A normal routine. But there was something flat in Emma's tone and a slump to her shoulders that was so uncharacteristic that Tom guessed she was very upset about something.

It was possible that Emma had also had a bad day at work. Awful things could happen in emergency departments. A child could have died, perhaps. Emma could just have pushed herself too hard and was feeling tired and sore

But the knot that formed in Tom's stomach and killed any appetite he might have had for the delicious food Emma had prepared could only be there because he knew, instinctively, that whatever was upsetting Emma was going to have a very personal effect on himself.

It had something to do with Simon Flinders.

Bathing Mickey, getting him into bed and reading him the obligatory story took more than an hour. An hour in which Tom tried to eat but then abandoned his dinner. Tried to watch the news on television and gave up because it held no interest. By the time Emma came into the living room and closed the hallway door behind her, Tom was just sitting on the couch, nursing a can of beer and letting his anxiety have free rein.

Emma looked up as she closed the door and Tom was struck by how pale she looked.

Pale…and sad. Almost fragile. The need to protect and comfort this woman was overpowering. It conquered any selfish need for comfort himself.

'Come and sit down,' Tom invited. 'You look done in.'

'I'm OK.' But Emma obediently crossed the room and sat down. Not on the single armchair she usually favoured in the evenings but on the couch beside Tom. 'Mickey's sound asleep,' she said.

'Is he all right?'

'He's fine. He had a great day at the centre. He's got a new best friend, apparently, called Timmy. They had a huge water fight and needed a complete change of clothes this afternoon.'

Tom listened to the forced brightness in Emma's tone. She was attempting to cover up whatever was really filling her mind. While he admired her courage, he wasn't going to let her deal with it on her own.

'Would you like a cup of coffee?' Emma asked. 'You don't seem to be drinking that beer.'

'No, I'm not. But I don't really want a coffee

either, thanks.' Tom put the can down. 'I want you to tell me what's wrong, Em.'

Her face stilled. 'What makes you think something's wrong?'

She might have pulled off some kind of denial if she hadn't looked up. Tom just held her with his gaze, communicating his conviction that she was upset. Hopefully the message of his desire to understand and help would get through as clearly.

It seemed to. Emma's eyes filled with tears. She blinked furiously but a single fat drop escaped and, without thinking, Tom reached out and brushed it from her cheek with his thumb.

And then he was holding Emma in his arms, just the way he had dreamed of doing. His fantasies hadn't included her shaking with silent sobs but that was OK. Tom was happy to hold her. To stroke her back and wait for as long as it took for a chance to listen.

It didn't take long. Emma pulled herself together and sat up, escaping the circle of Tom's arms.

'Sorry.'

'Don't be.' Tom waited a few more seconds while Emma wiped her face with her hands and sniffed away the last of her tears. 'What's wrong?' he queried again gently. 'Has this got something to do with Simon?'

Emma nodded miserably.

'You saw him?'

Another slow nod. 'I bumped into him in the car park.'

'And?' Tom's heart skipped a beat. Emma wouldn't be looking this miserable if the meeting had gone well. Part of him wanted to punch the creep for upsetting her like this but another part couldn't help a mix of relief and even hope making an appearance.

'And he was horrible,' Emma said.

'He wasn't pleased to see you?'

'Oh, he was pleased enough at first—after he got over the surprise factor. But then I told him about Mickey.' Emma sighed deeply. 'It was stupid. Of course it must have been a shock. I wasn't exactly diplomatic either. He...he actually had the nerve to sound sur-prised that I'd gone through with the pregnancy. And then to ask if I was sure Mickey was his.' She gave an incredulous snort. 'OK, I was twenty-two when I met Simon but I was still a virgin. He *knew* that.'

Tom had to suppress a flash of pure fury. He could understand Simon being attracted to Emma only too well, but for an older, *married* man to take advantage of a young, inexperienced girl like that was unforgivable.

Any unease regarding Emma's morality in keeping Mickey's birth hidden from his father evaporated. Simon had used her and broken her heart. Maybe Emma had been right to take the path she had chosen. Simon hadn't deserved to know he had a cute son like Mickey.

'He thinks I've come after him for financial support or something. He's in the middle of sorting out a messy divorce and he doesn't want the complication that Mickey and I represent. He made it very clear that he expected me to keep this private. He said I'd regret it if I didn't. Maybe he would make sure I lost my job.'

'He couldn't do that.'

'I imagine he could make life a bit difficult if he wanted to. What if he decided he wanted some kind of access or custody agreement?'

'We'd make sure he didn't succeed.'

'Simon could afford the best legal advice. People like that usually get what they want.' Emma closed her eyes. 'It's not as if I have any intention of telling anybody, anyway. I don't want anyone knowing that Simon is Mickey's father. I'm not even sure I want Mickey to know any more. He's…he's not the man I remembered.'

'It was a long time ago,' Tom pointed out. 'You were very young and you didn't know him for very long.'

'No.' It was a sad word. Was Emma letting go of something cherished? Realising that any love she'd had for Simon had been misplaced?

Tom knew he should give her some space to deal with whatever emotion she was experiencing but as the seconds ticked by it became unbearable to wait.

'Is there anything I could do to help?' he asked softly.

'You've helped heaps, Tom. Just being able to talk to you was just what I needed. Thank you.'

'No need to thank me,' Tom said. 'I'll always be here if you need me, Em.' He looked into Emma's face and had to fight with himself not to gather her into his arms again. How low would that be, to take advantage of her when she was upset and probably feeling lost? She must have harboured hopes of things working out with Simon to have come this far, and that dream had just been shattered. If Tom held her now, he might not be able to stop himself kissing her and that would make him no better than Simon.

'You're a great friend, Tom.' Emma's smile was watery but at least it appeared. Her gaze clung to him and to Tom's horror, he saw tears forming once more. Her voice was no more than a whisper. 'Could…could I have another hug, please?'

Wordlessly, Tom pulled her close. As if he could refuse such a request! He had no idea of how long they stayed like that. Tom basked in the sensation of holding Emma, of being able to comfort and protect her. Of almost drowning in the scent of her hair and skin and the warmth from her body.

And when she turned her face up and reached to touch his cheek, the invitation was totally irresistible. Tom bent his head and touched her lips with his own.

Just a brief, soft kiss. The sort of kiss a friend would bestow in time of great need.

It was the hardest thing Tom had ever done to lift his head and break that kiss before it became something unacceptable, but he managed to do it. Just.

And then he made the mistake of opening his eyes to see Emma staring at him, her dark eyes wide and vulnerable. He felt her hand tighten beneath his shoulder.

'I need more than a friend right now, Tom,' Emma said softly. 'Take me to bed. Please?'

Tom groaned. 'I can't do that, Emma.'

'Why not?'

'You're upset right now. I'd be taking advantage of you. It would complicate things for both of us.'

'Maybe it would make things clearer.' Tom could see the muscles in Emma's throat move as she swallowed. He wanted to press his lips to that spot on her neck where her heartbeat also showed. 'I don't just want to go to bed with you because I've had a bad day, Tom.' Emma ran the tip of a very pink tongue over her lips. 'I…want *you*.'

That declaration undid Tom completely. Or perhaps it was the sight of that tongue tip and the desire that darkened Emma's eyes until they appeared totally black.

Whatever.

When Tom kissed Emma again there was no hope of holding anything back. He knew that would be the case even as he was lowering his head towards her face, but what did it matter? Emma wanted this as much as he did. Her hand was on the back of his head, urging him forward.

Her lips were parted and when Tom felt the touch of her tongue against his, he was utterly lost. He had to run on instinct from then on and it seemed to serve him just fine, judging by the small sounds of pleasure that came from Emma.

A short time later, Tom got up from the couch with Emma still in his arms. He carried her into his bedroom and quietly nudged the door closed behind him with his foot.

CHAPTER SEVEN

ANY pain that might have been expected in the aftermath of a broken dream faded remarkably swiftly.

Emma didn't need Simon in her life. Didn't want him. Especially not now, when this new phase of her relationship with Tom had coloured her life with the hope of permanent happiness.

She was confident this hadn't happened simply because she had been in need of the comfort Tom could provide or the reassurance that she was attractive in the wake of any hurtful comments or attitude from Simon. The seeds of this relationship had been planted long ago—when Tom had laid his life on the line to save both Mickey and herself.

Mickey had no need of his birth father in his

life either. He was as happy as Emma had ever known him to be. If he'd noticed that his mother was no longer using the other single bed in his room, he made no comment. Emma had always been up earlier and had gone to bed much later so it was possible that the change had not yet registered. Mickey certainly noticed instantly if Max wasn't lying beside his bed ready to watch over him as he slept. When the small boy woke each morning and saw Max waiting to start the new day with him, his face would crinkle into the broadest smile possible.

Everybody seemed to be smiling a lot in Tom's house these days and Emma revelled in the cause. Tom's love-making was as wonderful as everything else about him. She had discovered a depth to a relationship that she hadn't believed possible.

This wasn't just physical attraction, the way it had been with Simon. And it certainly wasn't just having the basis of a close friendship that made it new. Somehow the two factors melded to produce a total that was infinitely greater than the sum the components should have been able to produce.

It was magic.

So was the way the happiness seemed to spread itself around. Phoebe noticed within a week that something had changed between Tom and Emma. She managed to restrain herself from commenting while they were sharing an evening meal but she was clearly excited and kept Mickey amused with incessant chatter.

'I'm going to Australia soon,' she told him. 'I'm having a holiday with my flatmates. Shall I bring you back a kangaroo?'

'What's a kangaroo?'

'A big animal that jumps and it has a pocket in its tummy.'

'What for?'

'To keep its lunch in, of course.'

Tom pointed his fork at his sister. 'Let's try and keep things at least partly accurate, Phoebs. You're warping an impressionable mind here.'

'The pouch is for the baby kangaroo to live in,' Emma said. 'We'll find a book about it.'

'There's lunch in there for the baby kangaroo,' Phoebe said in a stage whisper to Mickey. 'Honest!'

'You're all set for your holiday, then?' Tom asked.

'Almost. We've just got to find someone to feed the cat and water all the plants.'

'Get Mum to do it,' Tom suggested. 'Or I could.'

'I don't trust you,' Phoebe informed him cheerfully. 'And Mum hates driving all the way across town. We'll come back to find everything's dead.'

'I'll do it,' Emma offered. 'I know where you live.'

'Oh, would you?' Phoebe's face lit up. 'That would be fantastic. Are you sure you wouldn't mind?'

'Of course not. You've been wonderful to me and Mickey. I'd be delighted to be able to help.'

'Sold,' Phoebe declared. 'To the highest bidder.' She watched as Tom cleared their empty plates and moved to the sink. Then her gaze moved purposefully back to Emma. 'Are you two…you know…?'

The meaningful tilt of her head towards her brother's back made the subject of her question unmistakable. Emma was thankful that Tom swung around before she could decide how best to respond.

'Yes,' he told Phoebe. He gave her an equally meaningful headshake with the direction of his gaze reminding her that Mickey was still at the table.

Phoebe beamed at Emma. 'Excellent! So you'll be coming to Mum's for family dinner on Sunday?'

'Um…' Would Tom want to take the step of drawing her closer to his family? It seemed like a significant step.

'Would you like to come, Em?' Tom's tone was deceptively casual and his expression was unreadable.

Yes. This was a step forward and Emma felt suddenly nervous. While Tom seemed as happy as she had been in the last week with the development between them, their relationship was still very new and possibly fragile. He hadn't made any reference to future plans and Emma wasn't about to broach the subject. This was a time for enjoying each day as it came. Cementing the new bond they had without putting undue pressure on it.

'If it's not going to be a big deal for your mum,' Emma said a little ambiguously, 'that would be lovely.'

'I want to come, too,' Mickey said.

'Of course you can come.' Phoebe nodded. 'My mum's kept every toy we ever had when we were kids. They're all in boxes, just waiting for a little boy to come and play with them.' She grinned at Tom. 'This might even let us off the hook about producing umpteen grandchildren in the foreseeable future.'

Emma saw the look that passed between the siblings and a faint warning bell sounded in the back of her mind as Tom resumed rinsing the dinner dishes. She remembered Tom's relieved reference to having avoided children so far in his life. He seemed more than happy to accept Mickey but if they stayed together, did that mean her son would never have even half-siblings?

Did that matter?

Did loving someone the way Emma suspected she loved Tom have to automatically include having a baby together? Judging by the disappointment that threatened to spoil the mood of the evening, it seemed to. It was one of probably many things that she and Tom would have to talk about. When the time was right, though, and that certainly wasn't right now.

'Can Max come, too?' Mickey was demanding.

'No.' Tom shook his head firmly. 'Sorry, Mickey, but Mum's got a little white dog that hates Max. She tries to bite him.'

Mickey looked alarmed. 'Will she try to bite me, too?'

'No way, kiddo.' Phoebe stood up and bent down to Mickey's chair. 'Don't you worry. If it even shows its teeth, I'll turn it into a fluffy white football and kick it out the door.'

'Phoebe!' Tom chided.

But Mickey was giggling and holding his

arms up to be carried. 'Playtime,' he ordered Phoebe.

She picked him up and grinned at Emma over the child's shoulder. 'I won't hype him up too much before bedtime, I promise.'

'That's cool.'

'And thanks so much for the offer to feed the cat and stuff. You're great.'

'It'll be a pleasure.'

'I'll give you a key when I see you at Mum's on Sunday.'

Tom filled the kettle and plugged it in. 'You sure about Sunday, Em? You want to meet my mother and her horrible little dog?'

Emma smiled and kept her tone light. 'Only if you're happy about it, Tom.'

Tom didn't smile back but Emma could read the warmth in his eyes. 'I'd love you to come,' he assured her. 'Mum's going to be so pleased to finally meet you. *And* Mickey.'

Jan Gardiner was indeed delighted to welcome Emma and her son. The family heirloom toys were a huge success and by the end of the evening Mickey was calling Tom's mother 'Nanna' and Jan was begging Emma to let her care for Mickey on at least some of the occasions he would normally go to the day-care centre.

'I know he has friends there,' she said, 'but I have friends who meet when they've got their grandchildren for the day and I've been dying to be included!'

Tom and Phoebe rolled their eyes behind her back but Emma seemed happy to take the offer on board and Mickey was only too pleased with the prospect of opening the boxes of toys again.

Phoebe gave Tom yet another significant look which Tom ignored. OK, so Emma seemed to like his mother and Mickey had been a cute addition to the regular family gathering, but that didn't mean he had to propose to Emma immediately, did it?

It wasn't as if he wasn't *thinking* about doing exactly that. Rather too much, in fact. The desire to weave Emma and her son into his life on a permanent basis had been fierce ever since he had woken up that morning with the utter contentment of finding Emma still in his bed.

Repeating the astonishing pleasure of making love to Emma wasn't diminishing the excitement and satisfaction Tom experienced. If anything, it just got better and better. It was infusing his whole life. He couldn't stop smiling and everyone noticed.

'You look happy,' Josh told him accusingly.

'I *am* happy,' Tom admitted. 'Is that a problem?'

'The weather's awful. We've just had a callout to a boat rescue and a winch job is not going to be fun in these conditions. You can't be that happy.'

'Well, I am.'

'Fine. You can do the dangling, then. You won't look so happy if you break your leg, landing on a rough deck.'

'I'm not so sure about that.' Tom couldn't resist teasing Josh by grinning broadly. 'But I'm happy to do the winch and I won't break my leg. You can stay nice and dry in the chopper.'

Josh handed him the harness. 'Cool.' He zipped up his overalls over the thermal undergarments they needed for a job at sea.

'It's that woman, isn't it? The one who's living with you.'

'What is?'

'The reason you're looking so damned pleased with yourself all the time.'

'Could be.' Tom jammed his helmet on and followed Josh towards the helicopter pad. His smile was inward this time because he didn't want to irritate his partner any further. 'Could well be.'

Winching onto a relatively small yacht on a moderately heavy sea was certainly not fun. It was fraught. Fortunately there were enough people on board the pleasure craft to help make the process a little safer.

A weighted 'Hi-line' was deployed first from the helicopter and the skipper of the yacht knew not to attach it to any part of his vessel.

Tom attached a supply kit and nappy harness to an extension on the winch hook. It would be a lot faster to evacuate their patient with the harness rather than a stretcher, and from the information they'd been given it sounded like the middle-aged man had suffered a heart attack. He had severe chest pain and nausea. He might have had heart failure going on already by the sound of symptoms like swollen ankles and difficulty breathing. The sooner they could get him on board the helicopter and on the way to hospital, the better.

Emma was working today as well, so a trip to transfer a patient to the emergency department was more than welcome as far as Tom was concerned. He loved seeing her at work. Checking the attachment to the items he was carrying before he leaned out on the skids, Tom had another reminder of Emma. The last time he had used a nappy harness had been during her rescue.

It had been way too big for Mickey. He'd ended up holding his tiny victim during that rather unconventional rescue mission. Tom could remember the feel of holding him very clearly. Was that because the rescue had been so dangerous or was it because he was so used to picking the small boy up and carrying him around now? So used to hearing that infectious gurgle of laughter and living in the chaos and noise children could create. His house would seem dead without Mickey now.

Maybe he and Emma could have some children of their own. Brothers and sisters for Mickey. Tom was sure Mickey would love that. And Max would be in heaven, but this was not the time to be thinking in terms of anything more than the very immediate future. The deck of the yacht was looming steadily nearer, rolling with the sea, which made the wooden deck recede and then move upwards again in a disconcerting fashion.

'Minus twenty…' he told Josh as he estimated the distance left to travel downwards. 'Fifteen…'

'Back and left to target,' he heard Josh telling Terry, the pilot.

The weighted line that had been initially deployed from the helicopter was used to pull Tom in slowly from where he hung a safe distance from the side of the boat, timing the final part of his descent with care.

'Minus four,' he warned Josh. 'Wait for the next wave… Right, minus three…two…' And then his feet connected to the deck and he staggered forward, reaching to unclip his winch hook at the same time.

'Where's the patient?' he asked the skipper. 'And is he still conscious?'

'Yes, but he's not looking too flash.'

'What's his name?'

'John.'

Tom eased his gear through the door to the sleeping compartment. 'Hey, John, I'm Tom,' he introduced himself. 'How are you feeling?'

'Not so good.'

Tom was still adjusting to the dimmer light of the yacht's cabin. 'Have you got any history of cardiac problems?'

'No. Never had a sick day in my life.'

'You're forty-nine, yes?'

'Yes.'

'How's your breathing at the moment?'

'I'm feeling pretty puffed.'

Tom could see the rapid respiratory rate his patient's chest movement was advertising. With his fingers on John's wrist he could also feel how hard his heart was working. And he noticed something else.

'Have you been scuba-diving in the last forty-eight hours, John?'

'Yes.'

'We all went diving.' John's wife was sitting on the opposite bunk. 'That's what this cruise has been about. We've been down almost every day. Nothing too deep and the last dive was only to about fifteen metres.'

'DCI can occur even during shallow dives,' Tom said. 'We certainly can't rule it out as a cause for John's symptoms.' He looked again at the mottled skin on his patient's arm. 'Is your skin itchy?'

'It's driving me nuts.'

'How long has it been this blotchy?'

'Is it?' John lifted his arm. 'I hadn't noticed. Mind you, my eyes don't feel right.'

'In what way?'

'Everything's kinda blurry.'

The chest pain and nausea could well have a cardiac cause. So could the swollen ankles and difficulty breathing but mottled, itchy skin didn't fit. Decompression sickness was more likely. Tom spoke to Josh through his radio.

'We need the stretcher down here, mate. I don't want to position John upright in the harness. Looks like DCI.'

He turned to the skipper. 'I'll need your help. We'll have to send the lines down again and bring a stretcher on board.'

'Isn't it more important to get John away to hospital?' his wife asked anxiously. 'It's going to take a lot more time with the stretcher, isn't it?'

'It's important we keep John completely flat.'

'Why?'

'Did they teach you about decompression sickness in the diving course you did?'

'I guess. I don't remember.'

'Well, the reason people get sick is that the gases they breathe underwater get absorbed into the bloodstream. Nitrogen gets transformed into little bubbles as the diver comes up to the surface and those bubbles can lodge in body tissues and enter the bloodstream.'

'But we didn't come up too quickly. We followed all the rules really carefully.'

'Yeah. We sure did.' The skipper was looking as worried as John's wife, now.

'It can happen anyway,' Tom told them. 'And the reason we need to keep John flat and use the stretcher is to stop any of those nitrogen bubbles getting into his brain.' He listened to the message he was receiving and nodded at the yacht's skipper. 'Josh is sending down the stretcher. I'm going to get some oxygen going for John and then we'll go and get it.'

High-flow oxygen was the main treatment Tom could offer his patient until they could get him to a hyperbaric chamber. IV fluids were also important to counteract the damage nitrogen bubbles in the bloodstream could be causing. Apart from that, there was little Tom could do apart from giving pain relief. He would be happier once he was on board the helicopter and could add cardiac monitoring to his investigations, but he was confident they were dealing with a case of the 'bends.'

And that meant they had an issue in flying

John to hospital. An altitude of greater than three hundred metres above sea level could exacerbate the condition by making the gas bubbles expand, but flying really low was only possible until they got to shore.

'We'll need road back-up,' Tom warned Terry. 'Can you co-ordinate landing at the nearest beach to the hospital?'

'Sure. No problem.'

And it wasn't a problem. Just a disappointment because it meant that Tom would be handing over their patient to a road-based crew and he wouldn't have any time in the emergency department on this job. He'd probably have to wait until he got home to see Emma again.

It was on the beach, a commendably short time later, when Tom watched the ambulance pull away with its beacons flashing, that the desire to see Emma became unbearably powerful.

Not just to catch a moment or two during working hours, to share a look or a smile that no one else could share. Tom wanted to see Emma every day…for the rest of his life.

He wanted to make a commitment. To let her

know how much he loved her. To find the only way he could think of that could offer some security for their future together.

Tom was going to ask Emma to marry him. Today.

As soon as he finished his shift.

Emma was rostered on until a little later than he was for once and Tom had already arranged to collect her from the hospital. With a bit of luck they would have enough time together on their way to pick up Mickey for Tom to tell Emma exactly how he felt about her.

To propose marriage for the first, and hopefully only, time in his life.

Being nervous about taking such a big step was only to be expected, but Tom was surprised by his level of trepidation by the time he walked into ED a little after 6 p.m.

What if Emma said no? If she needed more time to trust him and what they had together? What if this relationship was a rebound phenomenon for her and she still hadn't given up on Mickey's father?

Emma was nowhere to be seen in the department, which served to fuel Tom's nervousness. It wasn't until he spotted her coming from the direction of the sluice room that the knot in his gut began to loosen. When she saw him waiting, Emma's face lit up with surprise and then pleasure and she smiled at him so happily Tom felt a wash of love that took him to a place he'd never been before. He knew his plan of action was the right one to take.

The only one.

And surely he couldn't feel this strongly if he had any genuine reason to doubt that Emma felt the same way.

Tom smiled back. He waited until she was close enough for any conversation they might have to be private and then he broke their unspoken rule of not making their relationship too obvious during working hours.

'Hey, babe,' he said softly. 'Fancy a ride home?'

Emma paused, standing close enough to Tom for them to be almost touching.

'Sure do,' she murmured, 'but I can't leave

just yet.' She was holding Tom's gaze and her expression was apologetic. 'I've got a really sick young girl in Resus 2. Paige, her name is. She came in with sudden onset hemiplegia and the CT has shown up a rather nasty-looking high spinal tumour. They're taking her to Theatre any time now but I promised I'd go upstairs with her.'

'I'll wait for you.'

Appreciation flashed in Emma's dark eyes. 'I was hoping to be ready to leave on time. I thought we might be able to go out for a quick drink or something before we collect Mickey.'

It sounded perfect to Tom. A quiet bar and a glass of champagne could create a very appropriate ambience.

He just wished Emma looked a bit happier, but he could understand why she didn't. A serious diagnosis in a young patient she had probably formed a bond with was more than enough to create the anxiety he could now read in her eyes. Tom searched her face, trying to gauge whether Emma might, in fact, be so upset about this case that it would make it a bad time to propose.

'It's not the time so much that I mind,' Emma added quickly. 'The surgeon's coming to talk to Paige and her parents before they move her.' It was more than anxiety Tom could see now. It was almost fear. 'It's Simon's firm that's on call.'

'He can't hurt you, Em,' Tom said with quiet authority. 'I wouldn't let him.'

By way of further reassurance, Tom leaned even closer to Emma so that they *were* touching as he bent his head to make sure she could hear him.

Emma nodded and then moved away with obvious reluctance. Tom watched her slip between the curtains screening Resus 2. He stared at the space she had left empty on his side of the curtains for several seconds and then he sighed and turned away.

To find himself under the intense scrutiny of Simon Flinders.

The stare was not a pleasant one.

No wonder Emma was tense at the prospect of another encounter with this man. Tom found himself straightening, his face settling into lines of a surprisingly grim determination to hold his position—both physical and moral—until Mickey's father walked past in order to get to his waiting patient. It was quite possible that Tom would have to have dealings with the surgeon in the future, because of his relationship to Mickey, and something told him he'd better make it clear that he wasn't easily intimidated.

He expected Simon to simply ignore him as he walked past to enter Resus 2.

But he didn't walk past. He stopped. His gaze flicked over Tom's paramedic insignia on his uniform and clearly dismissed his ranking in the medical profession. His voice was low enough to be perfectly discreet.

'Bit of all right, isn't she?'

'Sorry?'

Simon's well-groomed head nodded at where Emma had last been seen. Not that Tom had any doubt who the surgeon was referring to. He had just found such a startlingly unprofessional comment unbelievable.

'Know Emma well, do you?'

Tom's response dripped ice. 'Yes.'

Simon smiled. 'So do I. We go way back.'

'Yes.' Tom managed to sound as though the information was irrelevant, even while he could feel his blood pressure rising. 'So I believe.'

'I'm so pleased to find she's started working here.' Simon stared thoughtfully at the curtain around Resus 2. 'It'll give us a chance to renew our acquaintanceship.'

Tom couldn't let him get away with it. He needed to stand his ground for all sorts of reasons but mainly to protect Emma. Not that he believed she would want anything more to do with Simon, but the thought of her being upset again was enough.

Especially today.

How could Tom propose to the woman he loved if her mind was poisoned by thoughts of an ex-lover?

'Emma has no interest in renewing any acquaintance,' he found himself telling Simon. 'I'd suggest you leave her alone.'

How inappropriate was this? Two men, one of whom had urgent professional duties elsewhere, facing each other in an emergency department walkway, declaring their interests in the same woman.

Tom had the horrible thought that this was happening because of sheer bad luck in timing. If he hadn't been standing right here and hadn't broken the rules about personal contact with Emma at work, would Simon be staking any kind of a claim?

Tom doubted it. He had the impression that speaking like this was well out of character for the surgeon. That he had broken some rigidly held personal rules of his own because the provocation had been too great to resist. It was that undercurrent of such powerful emotion that disturbed Tom more than anything about this astonishing encounter.

Did Simon really care about Emma? Had he genuinely loved her years ago or was he simply the kind of man who liked to win? How deeply did having Emma walk out on him still rankle? Maybe seeing her with another man had been enough to spark renewed interest that could well be dangerous.

'I think we could leave that decision up to

Emma, don't you?' Simon's smile had vanished but the fresh quirk of his lips suggested confidence. 'We have, if you like, an interest in common?'

Mickey. The bastard was planning to use Emma's son as a pawn.

It was probably just as well Tom didn't have a chance to respond. Simon moved on as smoothly as he had arrived. He twitched the curtain to Resus 2 and went in without a backward glance.

He came out only minutes later, completely ignoring Tom as he left the department with a purposeful stride. Then the bed carrying Paige emerged, surrounded by attendant medical staff and a bank of monitoring equipment. Emma was walking beside the young girl, holding her hand. The parents walked behind the head of the bed, clutching each other's hands.

Emma glanced at Tom but her half-smile was distracted and no wonder, judging by the terrified faces of the family she was accompanying. The double doors into the hospital's interior slid open and the entourage vanished.

Heading towards Theatre where Simon was waiting for them all.

And that was all Tom could do as well.

Wait.

CHAPTER EIGHT

THE plight of her patient had touched Emma deeply.

That was probably why she was responsive to the apparently genuine appeal from Paige's surgeon, who seemed determined to use the few spare minutes he had before scrubbing in to talk to Emma.

'I want to apologise,' he told her quietly. 'And we *do* need to talk, don't we?'

There was no disputing that. The question of whether Mickey would ever meet his birth father still hung over Emma and clouded any dreams she might have for a future with Tom. You couldn't move on until you had at least sorted the past in your own head, could you? Unless you had some idea what might influence the future?

Paige was now under the care of the anaesthetist. Orderlies removed the emergency department's bed and one of Emma's colleagues ushered Paige's parents in the direction of the relatives' waiting area. The theatre staff were all busy, preparing for the emergent and probably complex surgery that would start soon but the normal scheduled activity for the day had ceased and the holding bay for expected patients was an oasis of calm. It was to this relatively private place that Simon led Emma.

'I really am sorry,' he said without preamble. 'You took me completely by surprise, Emma, but that's no excuse for behaving like such an idiot. You'd think I was old enough to know better, wouldn't you?' The charm evident in the self-recrimination was very familiar but it didn't work the kind of magic it once had.

'It doesn't matter, Simon. I'm over it.' Over you, Emma added silently. There had been a brief moment, back in Resus 2, when Simon had entered wearing his theatre scrubs when Emma had experienced another one of those flashbacks and could remember very clearly how attractive she had found him that first time she'd seen him in action. The clothing advertised his status and was shapeless enough to accentuate the symmetry of a very handsome face.

And then Emma had emerged to see Tom in *his* uniform. With a rugged kind of face that could not compete with the bone structure of male models. And Simon suddenly seemed plastic. As superficial as Emma's instincts warned her he had probably always been.

She wasn't about to tell Simon how she felt about him now, however. She hadn't forgotten the fear he had instilled by his implied threat. A man of his position could well find some way to disrupt her life by laying claim to his son.

'It matters to me,' Simon said. 'A lot.' He smoothed an imaginary crinkle in the cover of one of the holding-bay beds and then sat down. Sideways, with one leg hooked up. He looked far less intimidating as Emma looked down at him and she declined the hand waved invitation to sit on the end of the bed.

'Things are changing for me, Emma,' Simon

continued. 'I think fate might have dropped you back into my life with admirable timing.'

'That's not the impression I got the other day, Simon.'

'No. And I've apologised for that. Sincerely, I hope.'

Emma ducked her head in acknowledgement.

'I lost my court case this week. If I move to the States—to the job I would be crazy to turn down—I may not see very much of my children until they're old enough to leave home and choose for themselves. It's not a happy position to be in.'

'No, I don't suppose it is.' What if Simon had had custody of *their* son and had lived on the other side of the world? The ongoing ache of loss would be unbearable. There was no reason to think that Simon didn't love his children any less than she loved Mickey.

Simon seemed to be reading her thoughts. 'I love my children,' he said softly. 'I know I haven't been the best father in terms of the time I've had available, but I've provided for them in the best way I could. I can't believe how distressing the thought of losing contact with them is proving.'

Emma said nothing. He didn't *have* to move to the States, did he? He could stay in Christchurch and be a weekend dad. But if he did that, and if things worked out between herself and Tom, they could all be living in the same city—and how would that work? Would she have to give up Mickey every second weekend as well? The notion was very unappealing.

'At least one good thing has come out of a horrendous period for me,' Simon said. 'I can see now that the surprise of finding I have another son is a gift rather than an unwelcome complication.'

Emma still said nothing. A feeling of dread was beginning to form.

'I could legally claim parental rights.' Simon was still looking up at Emma and his confident tone was tempered by a tentative smile. 'But I don't suppose you travelled twelve thousand miles if you had the intention of contesting those rights, did you?'

'It depends on what rights you're talking

about,' Emma said. She wasn't going to let Simon have regular or prolonged access to her son. Not now, when she knew there was no chance she would want to be with Simon again herself.

'I wouldn't ask for anything that you're not happy about,' Simon reassured her. 'All I'm asking for right now is the opportunity to meet my son. For him to meet his father.'

Which was precisely what Emma had planned when she had decided to make this journey. She searched Simon's face, still upturned, his blue eyes shining in appeal, and failed to detect a lack of sincerity.

She believed him.

Maybe it would be possible for them to end up being friends. To share, in some way, the joy of the child they had created together. Maybe her old fantasies had gone up in a puff of smoke but this one had a grounding in reality, didn't it? And wouldn't it be the best thing possible for everyone involved? Especially Mickey?

'Mr Flinders?' A nurse appeared through the

swing doors of the operating theatre suite. 'We're ready for you.'

Simon stood up. 'I have to go.'

Emma nodded. 'Will Paige be all right, do you think?'

'I hope so.' Simon's face creased into an empathetic frown. 'It's a pretty nasty thing to have discovered but I'll be doing my best to make sure the damage is minimised. We'll just have to keep our fingers crossed that the tumour's not malignant.'

The surgeon's focus was now very appropriately fastened on the case ahead of him and his expression suggested that a good outcome was just as important to him as it was to Emma. Some of the respect she had once felt for Simon returned.

He hadn't totally forgotten about her, though. He turned back just before he pushed the swing doors open.

'Think about it, Emma. Please.'

Tom checked his watch for the umpteenth time.

What could be taking so long? He'd been

waiting for nearly half an hour now. He and Emma wouldn't be able to stop for that drink on the way home and proposing while negotiating rush-hour traffic was hardly romantic. Having summoned the courage to do something so life-altering, it was hugely disappointing to have to concede that a postponement was inevitable.

The disappointment evaporated on seeing Emma rush through the doors.

'I'm so sorry, Tom. I got held up.'

'Not a problem. Shall we get going?'

'I'll just grab my bag.' Emma still looked apologetic. 'I don't suppose we've got time for that drink now, have we?'

'Mickey's probably getting pretty hungry.' Tom followed Emma towards the locker room. 'Did you have to wait until Paige was asleep?'

'No. The anaesthetist team were great. I got held up by Simon, surprisingly. He wanted to talk. I'll be back in a sec and I'll tell you all about it.' Emma was leaving Tom to wait again as she disappeared into the locker room.

He hadn't found the information at all surprising. Not after the interchange he'd had with the surgeon in Emergency. He did find it deeply disturbing, however. What he needed as he and Emma walked towards the car park minutes later was some kind of reassurance that she hadn't been sucked in by Simon's new agenda.

And he wasn't getting it.

'You don't mind me talking about this, do you, Tom?'

'Of course not.'

'You seem kind of quiet.'

'I'm just listening. Simon seems to have persuaded you that meeting Mickey is a good thing.'

'Well, I'm not absolutely sure but I'm certainly going to have to think about it. I mean, he *is* Mickey's father. He does have rights.'

'Does he?' Tom jabbed the remote he was holding and the interior lights of his four-wheel-drive came on. He yanked open the driver's door.

Emma climbed into the passenger seat beside him and eyed him with a worried frown.

'You're not happy about this, are you?'

'No.'

'Why not?'

'Isn't it obvious? He's already upset you once. More than once. Maybe you were right. The dishonest way he treated you took away any rights he might have had.'

'That's not what you used to think. It was partly your disapproval over me never telling him that made me decide to stay and sort it out.'

'What disapproval? I've never said anything.'

'You didn't need to. I felt it the first time I met you. When I told you about Simon.' Emma shook her head impatiently at Tom's blank expression. 'In the van—when you were trying to pull that piece of metal out of my leg.'

Tom shook his head. All he remembered was the feeling of vague disappointment that Emma was in the country with an agenda that included a man. A pale emotion compared to the churning in his gut that he was currently experiencing.

'And you were happy to let me stay with you

when you knew I was waiting for Simon to get back. You approved of my plan to hang around long enough for him to have a chance to get to know Mickey.'

Tom turned the ignition key. 'Maybe I had other reasons to approve of you hanging around.'

'Like what?'

'You know what.' The engine was running but Tom made no move to reverse out of the parking slot. 'I was attracted to you.' He turned to face her. 'More than attracted, Emma. I'd already fallen in love with you.'

'You knew I had baggage,' Emma said slowly. 'Any past relationship leaves baggage and one that involves a child has infinitely more. It's something we're going to have to deal with if there's any hope for us lasting long term.' She was staring at Tom in the half-light of dusk. 'I don't understand. If you were already in love with me when you knew I was planning to let Simon meet Mickey, why should it make any difference now that it's going to happen?'

'*Is* it?'

'Why shouldn't it?'

'Simon's just using Mickey, Emma. He's trying to get at you.'

'I didn't get that impression when I was talking to him. He seems to genuinely care that he has a child he's never met.'

I'll bet he does, Tom thought furiously. And he was probably very convincing or Emma wouldn't be sounding so defensive. Should he tell Emma about his own conversation with Simon? Would she believe that she was being manipulated and that Simon's relationship to Mickey was merely a useful ploy?

Instinct warned Tom that it was something Emma would have to discover for herself if she was going to believe it. However hard it might be for him to stay silent, it was important that he did so. Emma would see his attitude as interference and might assume it was an expression of jealousy, which was an unattractive feature in anybody.

It was quite possible that Tom could unconsciously aid Simon by sabotaging the trust he and Emma had been building. What they had already built looked alarmingly precarious at this moment in time. Had he really been planning to propose this evening? It looked very much as though they were sinking into their first-ever fight instead. Disappointment and frustration combined to create a deep sense of hurt that found a very limited outlet in action. Having cleared the car park, Tom put his foot on the accelerator. Emma looked startled at the speed they rapidly gained.

'Why do you dislike Simon so much?' she queried suddenly. 'You don't even know him.' Tom could feel Emma staring at his profile. 'I wouldn't have picked you for the jealous type, Tom. I'm beginning to feel like I don't know you as well as I thought.'

'I'm not the one who's done a U-turn here, Emma. It was only a couple of weeks ago that you were devastated by the way Simon had treated you. You were scared he was going to get you fired or something if you made the truth about his unwanted child public.'

'I took him by surprise. He was shocked.'

'Or maybe he was unguarded. Maybe that was the real Simon you were seeing.'

'I think I know him a bit better than you do, Tom.'

'You certainly do.'

Emma made an incredulous sound. 'I can't believe you're so angry about this. If you think I want it for *my* sake rather than Mickey's then you couldn't be more wrong. There's nothing for you to be jealous about.'

Tom had to slow and then stop for traffic lights. He turned his head sideways.

'Mickey thought I was his father,' he blurted. 'And you know what? It gave me a bit of a jolt at the time but when I'd got used to the idea I found I liked it. I could be a father to him. A *good* father.'

Emma opened her mouth to respond but Tom didn't give her the chance. 'He doesn't need another father figure in his life. It would confuse him.'

'But he knows that Simon exists. What his name is. One day he's going to want to know more.'

'So leave it until then.'

'I can't. Simon wants it now. He implied that

he could probably demand it legally, and he could be right for all I know.' Emma sighed deeply when Tom said nothing and the silence continued until he turned into the road where the day-care centre was situated.

'Simon's got other children, Tom. They're half-brothers and -sisters for Mickey. Maybe they'll be the closest thing to siblings he'll ever have, seeing as you aren't interested in having your own children.'

Tom applied the handbrake with far more force than necessary. They both jerked forward in their seat belts.

'Where the hell did *that* come from?' Tom couldn't believe this. Instead of them happily planning a future together in the wake of the marriage proposal he had hoped to make, Emma seemed to be doing her utmost to prove it could never work.

Maybe it was just as well he *hadn't* proposed.

'Oh, I don't know.' Emma's voice was tight. 'Perhaps it was when we were in the van and I asked whether you had kids and you sounded so relieved when you said you'd managed to avoid them so far.' She gave a soft snort. 'Or maybe it has something to do with the way you and Phoebe look so exasperated when your mother says anything about wanting grand-children.'

'But that's different!' Emma was quite right, he had said that. And he hadn't liked the pressure from his mother to settle down and have a family, but this *was* different. Tom wasn't quite sure why, he just knew it was. Probably because those hypothetical children or grandchildren had not had the prospect of having Emma as their mother. 'That was in the past,' he told Emma. 'That was the way it was before I met you.'

'You're saying you want children?'

'No.' Or was he? 'Yes.' Tom felt too hurt right now to know *how* he felt about the idea of having children. He cleared his throat. 'I don't know. And I don't understand why I have to decide right now. How did we get onto a subject like this anyway?'

'How would *you* feel if I had your child and went away and you never got to meet it?'

The thought of Emma pregnant with his baby and disappearing from his life was shocking. The thought of her leaving at all was shocking. But this wasn't about them. It was about letting Simon force his way into their lives. Making a claim on the most important part of Emma's life. Trying to win her back. Could Tom live with the kind of tension that would create?

Not happily, that was for sure.

'I hope you're not comparing me to Simon,' he snapped.

'I'm trying to explain why I have to go through with letting him meet Mickey even if neither of us are particularly happy about it. It's what I planned to do even before I booked the tickets to come to New Zealand. It's because of how guilty I've felt for years now about keeping my son a secret and why I can't continue to avoid the truth even if Simon was prepared to let me get away with it. Which I don't expect he is,' she added hurriedly. 'He just wants to meet his son, Tom. *His* son.'

A heavy silence fell. Tom stared sightlessly through the windscreen.

Was Emma trying to tell him that he would never be considered a father to Mickey? That he would just have to suck it in and put up with Emma and Simon spending time together as they shared bringing up their child? If Simon succeeded in convincing Emma that was what he wanted, just how long would it take for him to persuade her that they should all be together as one happy little family?

'If you want to meet Simon, I can't stop you,' he finally said heavily. 'But I'm not sure things can work between us if he's included in the equation.'

Emma gasped. 'Are you saying that if I go ahead with this, it's over between us?' She gave him no time to answer. 'I don't like ultimatums, Tom.'

'It's not an ultimatum. I just want you to know that I'm not happy about you seeing Simon.'

'No kidding?' There was a hint of sarcasm in Emma's tone that Tom had never heard before. He didn't like it. Neither did he like the belligerence that seemed to colour her next words. 'Why not? Don't you trust me?'

'I didn't say that.'

'Maybe you didn't need to. It's obvious. And if it isn't that you don't trust me, it's that you can't deal with my baggage. Either way, you might be right. I think we have a problem, Tom. A big problem.'

And with that, Emma pushed her door open and marched into the day-care centre to collect her son.

Max was looking worried. He lay on the kitchen floor, facing the back door, and whined softly.

'They've just gone to feed Phoebe's cat and water the plants,' Tom told his dog. 'They'll be back soon.'

Except they should have been back by now. When the phone rang, Tom guessed what had happened. The heavy atmosphere and the unresolved conflict had driven Emma away to find some space. How convenient that Phoebe's fully furnished flat was available. Had she thought of that before she'd set out to begin the responsibilities she had taken on or had the peace of a house that he wasn't in inspired the idea?

'Mickey and I are going to stay the night here,' Emma told him. 'Phoebe's cat hasn't come in for its dinner and it's getting a bit late. Mickey got tired so I put him to bed.'

'That's fine. See you tomorrow, then.'

'Um…maybe.' He could hear Emma's heavy sigh over the line. 'It might be a good idea if we have a day or two apart, Tom. A bit of thinking time.'

'A bit of talking time might be more useful.'

'We'll talk,' Emma promised, 'but I need to get my own head clear first. I've got to try and resolve past issues before I look too far ahead, Tom. Can you understand that?'

'Of course.'

'That has to include sorting out what, if any, place Simon has in Mickey's life.'

'So you're going to meet him?'

'I'll have to.'

'When?'

'I don't know. As soon as possible, I guess.'

How had things gone so wrong so quickly?

It was with a heavy heart that Emma collected some clean clothes from Tom's house the next day.

'But why do we have to stay at Phoebe's house again, Mummy?' Mickey had his arms around Max's neck and was looking mutinous.

'Because Fatso might run away from home if there's no one there and I promised Phoebe that we'd take care of him.'

'But I don't like Fatso. I like *Max*.'

'I know, darling, but it's not for long.'

'I could stay here. With Max. And Tom.'

'Tom has to go to work. He can't look after you all the time.'

'He looked after me all the time when you were sick.'

True. Where had that Tom gone? The one who had put himself out to such a degree to help her? Who'd taken on caring for a small, frightened, disabled boy when he hadn't known anything about children and hadn't been, according to his own confession, all that keen on having them around?

But he'd grown to like the idea of being Mickey's father. The warm glow that latest confession should have given Emma was buried under the weight of the tension surrounding her decision to introduce Simon to Mickey.

Emma was sure she was doing the right thing. It had to be done—for all sorts of reasons, not the least of which was her conviction that if what she and Tom had was going to last the distance, it would have to be able to cope with this kind of pressure. And she had to be allowed to do what was right for her. And for Mickey. She'd been as strong as she'd needed to be in the past for precisely that reason and it wasn't for Tom to decide what was important now.

He may well feel differently about it when it was a reality and not some kind of nebulous threat. When Emma could prove to him that she had no interest in Simon other than as Mickey's birth father.

So the sooner she got the initial meeting out of the way, the better. Then she could try and mend the rift that had escalated between herself and Tom. Thank goodness Simon seemed keen to co-operate. He'd even offered to take some time off work that very afternoon so that he could meet Emma and Mickey at a place of their choosing.

'There's a playground Mickey really likes,' Emma had suggested. 'Out near the airport in Black's Road. Would three o'clock be all right?'

There were other children at the popular playground that had become a favourite due to its easy walking distance from Tom's address. Emma pushed Mickey's wheelchair over to where a group was clambering over a mini-obstacle course.

'Want to get out of your chair to play?'

'No. I just want to watch.'

Emma wasn't surprised. There were no familiar faces among the children present that day and one of the boys was older and much bigger than Mickey. He had curly red hair and a lot of freckles and he exuded a confidence that Mickey certainly didn't possess.

'Why are you in that chair?' The red-headed boy lost no time in coming to investigate. 'Is there something wrong with your legs?'

'I can walk,' Mickey stated firmly. 'Just not for a long way yet.'

'Want me to push you?'

Mickey eyed the boy cautiously and Emma could see that shyness could get in the way of a new friendship.

'This is Mickey,' she told the boy. 'What's your name?'

'James.'

'You'll be careful if you push Mickey, won't you? The chair might tip over if you go too fast.'

James's mother was sitting on a nearby bench. 'He'll be careful,' she assured Emma. 'Won't you, Jamie?'

James nodded eagerly and Emma stepped back. It would be good for Mickey to make a new friend and, besides, she could see a man in a pinstriped suit approaching and she knew who it was. She moved to greet Simon.

'Emma! Good to see you again. Shall we find somewhere to sit down and talk?'

'Sure.' There was an unoccupied bench on the other side of the play area and Emma led the way. 'How did things go with Paige yesterday?' she queried.

'Fabulously well, if I'm allowed to be less than modest.' Simon tweaked up the legs of his trousers as he sat down. 'The tumour was benign, thank God, and I think we rescued the nerves before they suffered any permanent damage. Only time will tell, of course, but I'm confident she'll make a full recovery.'

'That's good news.'

Simon's nod was satisfied. He smiled. 'It's good to see you out of uniform, Emma. Did I tell you how great you're looking?'

He'd come here to see Mickey, not her. So why wasn't Simon even looking at any of the children? If it was Emma, she would be dead curious to see what a child of hers looked like.

As Simon's gaze returned to her face and Emma caught the glint in his eyes, she knew that Tom had been right. Simon was using Mickey to get to her. He still fancied her and she'd played right into his hands. She could see why Simon would wonder why she had agreed to meet him like this if she wasn't interested at some level.

'That's Mickey over there,' Emma said levelly. 'See?' She pointed to where James was pushing Mickey towards an exotic-looking climbing frame that was a series of interlocking circles.

'Really?' Simon frowned. 'He's big for his age, isn't he?'

'No. Small, actually.'

'Where did the red hair come from?'

'That's not Mickey.'

'Oh?' Simon turned his head and Emma stared at him. Was Mickey invisible because he was in a wheelchair? Or did it not occur to Simon that his child might have a disability because Emma hadn't thought to mention it?

'That's Mickey in the wheelchair,' she said a little nervously. *Why* hadn't she thought to mention it? If she wanted to protect Mickey from rejection she should have made sure that Simon knew in advance. Perhaps it was because they used the wheelchair so infrequently these days. The long walk to the park was about the only time Mickey needed the assistance. Any moment now he'd probably be climbing out of it to start playing with the other children.

Simon was obviously taken aback. 'He's in a wheelchair? What's wrong with him?'

'Spina bifida.'

'Oh? What level was the lesion?'

'L4 to 5.'

'What degree of disability has he got? Is he continent?'

'Getting there. And he's walking well with callipers now. He can even walk without them for short distances.'

Thanks to Max. And Phoebe.

'Hydrocephalus?'

'Minimal. He didn't need a shunt but he's been monitored carefully to make sure the fluid build-up didn't increase. As long as he doesn't get a head injury, it shouldn't be a problem.'

'What age did they do the surgery?'

'Twelve months.'

'Do you know what method they used?'

'Does it matter?' Emma had had enough of what seemed like a purely professional assessment of her son. This was his son that Simon was analysing in such a professional manner. 'He's a healthy, happy little boy, Simon. He loves to swim and build things and sing. And he loves dogs.'

And he doesn't like strange men coming into my life, Emma was tempted to add. She could see Mickey watching her from near the climbing frame. He had climbed out of his wheelchair and was holding onto one of the lower circles on the frame. James was way above him but Mickey was too busy looking at his mother to see his new friend waving. Even from this distance she could tell that her son's expression was deeply suspicious. He was bound to tell Simon to his face that he didn't like him if she took him over for an introduction. And how would she introduce him? Did Mickey remember her telling him the name of his 'real' father?

Emma needed a little time to decide how best to do this. Maybe it wouldn't even need to happen today. Simon might have a good idea about how and when he wanted to spend more time with Mickey.

But Simon was looking at his watch. 'I haven't got too much time, I'm afraid, Emma. I'll have to run in a few minutes.'

'Do you want to say hello to Mickey?'

'Ah...do you think that's a good idea?' Simon actually looked nervous and Emma felt a twinge of sympathy.

'We could leave it until next time, if you like.'

'That might be best. And maybe I could take you out to dinner in the meantime. You can tell me all about Mickey so I feel like I get to know him.'

'I don't want to have dinner with you, Simon. The best way to get to know Mickey is going to be to spend time with *him,* not me.'

Simon looked alarmed now. 'I don't want to spend time with him without you, Emma. I see this as a package deal, don't you?'

'What do you mean?'

'I'm planning to start a new life,' Simon said.

'I'm hoping that you and Mickey might be a big part of that. As I said, I've never forgotten you, Emma. I don't really think it was just a fling for either of us. I loved you. I think I still do.'

Emma was shaking her head. She'd always known, deep down, that Simon had never *really* loved her. If he had, he would have been honest with her right from the start. And he would have come looking for her when she run away. 'I'm not in love with you any more, Simon and…and I'm in a relationship with someone else now.'

At least, Emma *hoped* she still was. How stupid had it been to walk out instead of trying to talk it through? It really was a habit she needed to break.

'Someone I love very much.'

'That paramedic chap I saw you with yesterday?'

'Tom. Yes.'

'And you're sure about that?'

'Yes.'

So sure, in fact, that Emma couldn't remember why she thought it had been a good idea to have this meeting. No wonder Tom had been so upset. She hadn't even tried to see it from his point of view. And he'd been right. Simon wasn't interested in Mickey. Not enough, anyway. Her son would be far better off not knowing that.

'I think you should go, Simon.'

'What, you don't want me to even say hello to Mickey?'

'Not unless you're planning on being involved with his life. It's going to be pretty confusing for him if he gets introduced to a father who isn't around to even read an occasional story to him.'

'I'm happy to help, you know, financially.'

'I've already told you, I don't want your money.'

Simon didn't appear to be listening. He was staring over Emma's shoulder. 'Should he be doing that?'

'What?' Emma turned swiftly and then gasped. 'Oh…my God!'

Somehow Mickey had climbed to the top of the circular climbing frame. James was beside him and both boys were grinning at each other.

Emma was on her feet. *'Mickey!'* Her hoarse voice was almost inaudible.

Of course he shouldn't be doing that. He didn't have anywhere near enough strength in his lower body to climb safely. Emma wouldn't have believed he was capable of getting so far off the ground. She had assumed he was happy going round the bottom or she would never have taken her eyes off him. How long had it taken him to get so high? Over two metres!

He was looking so proud of himself. Emma tried not to run and panic her son. If she could just get there in time to get him down safely, he could celebrate his new achievement all he liked. She could just imagine him telling Tom all about it tonight. Tom would be—

'Look, Mummy! Look at *me*!'

Emma *was* looking. She saw the exact moment her precious little boy slipped and fell, hitting his head on every bar of the metal frame on the way down.

And then Emma started running, her scream trapped and resounding endlessly inside her head.

CHAPTER NINE

THE strident beeping of a high-priority callout on Tom's pager was a welcome distraction.

It didn't matter that it was a road-based job. The helicopter had been idle all day anyway, and at least he would be able to direct his thoughts away from himself for a while.

'Some kid's fallen off a jungle gym.' Josh had been inside the ambulance that was permanently stationed near the helipad and available for local calls if the SERT crew was not otherwise occupied. He pressed the button on the radio microphone he was still holding. 'Roger, got that. We're responding.' He slid into the passenger seat. 'You know where Black's Road is?'

Tom nodded. The V8 engine on the Mercedes ambulance roared into life and he flicked on the beacons.

'It's a long road. Want me to check the map and see where the playground is?'

'I know where it is.'

He'd been there. With Emma and Mickey. He'd pushed Mickey in one of the bucket-type swings and smiled at the shrieks of glee and gurgles of laughter the ride had elicited.

Maybe this job wasn't going to be enough of a distraction from a miserable day after all. Waking up in an empty bed, getting up to an empty house, watching Max ignore his breakfast had all been like some kind of punishment.

One that he had deserved.

Tom put his foot on the button that changed the siren's wail to a short, more urgent *yelp* as they approached the red lights of a major intersection. Cars edged sideways in the stationary lanes and traffic slewed to a halt from the lanes at right angles. A puff of smoke could be seen due to the over-rapid braking of a driver who had decided at the last minute that the emergency vehicle needed right of way.

Tom knew his miserable day was his own

fault. If he hadn't been so selfish yesterday, allowing his disappointment and jealousy to colour his judgement so badly, he could have supported Emma in what he knew was the right thing to do in letting Simon meet his son. Instead, his fear that he was going to lose, by painful degrees, what he wanted most had driven him into trying to throw it away instead. To try and put himself in a position of control—at least for the emotional fallout he knew he was at risk of experiencing.

In less than two minutes the ambulance arrived at the scene of the callout. Tom eased the vehicle over the kerb and drove across the grass towards the brightly coloured playground equipment. A cluster of people stood beside an improbable-looking climbing frame. A set of deserted bucket swings stood as a limp sentinels to one side.

Spotting an equally deserted small wheelchair should have alerted Tom to the personal nature of this call, but maybe he was so used to seeing one as part of the furniture, the connection failed to register.

With his focus on the crumpled form of a small child, still partially obscured by concerned onlookers, recognition of some of the adults present was also delayed.

'Can someone tell us what's happened?'

'The boy's fallen.' The man holding the boy's head still said. 'From this climbing frame.'

'Has he been moved since he fell?'

'Of course not.' The man looked up. 'Airway's clear. Breathing's OK but GCS is well down. I'd put it at 7 or 8. He's got a depressed skull fracture.'

'You a doctor, sir?' This from Josh who was positioning the portable oxygen cylinder and pulling a mask from the bag attached to its frame.

Tom crouched to deposit the life pack and kit he'd been carrying. No wonder the support for a cervical spine had looked so competent.

'This is Mr Flinders, Josh,' he said. 'He's a neurosurgeon.'

Tom glanced up only briefly. Just long enough to find the figure he knew had to be very close. Emma was kneeling on the other side of Mickey's head. Her face was deathly pale and she had her arms wrapped tightly around her own body. The dilemma she was grappling with was written all over her face. As a medical professional, she knew not to move a patient who had suffered a serious head and possibly a C-spine injury. As a mother, all she could think of doing was gathering her child into her arms to protect and comfort him.

Eyes that were dark pools of fear communicated too much. This was far worse for Emma than the terror of being trapped in that van. Right now she was facing an even closer reality of losing her son but surviving herself to live with the aftermath.

There was no more than a split second in which Tom could try and convey a promise of help. Then there was no time to spare to worry about Emma. Certainly no time to even form thoughts of any personal repercussions this accident could bring.

'How far did he fall?' Tom snapped on the beam of his penlight torch.

'A good two metres,' Simon informed him crisply. 'And he hit his head two, maybe three times on the way down.'

'Has he been responsive at all?'

'No.'

'Mickey?' Tom leaned close to the tiny, still face. 'Hey, buddy—it's Tom. Can you hear me? Can you open your eyes for me?'

There was a flicker of response. A twitch of eyelids and a faint moan that could have been an attempt to say something. It wasn't much but it was enough to elicit a stifled sob from Emma's direction.

Tom didn't look up. He drew back Mickey's eyelids and shone the beam of light onto his pupils.

'Right pupil unresponsive,' he said grimly. 'Dilated at four millimetres.' He moved the light to check behind Mickey's ears as Josh leaned in with the oxygen mask.

'No Battle's sign. Have you got that on at 15 litres?'

'Yes.'

A high level of oxygen was essential to try

and prevent secondary cerebral injury and, with this degree of unresponsiveness, Mickey was going to need intubation and ventilation.

He also need a neck collar and full spinal immobilisation before they could transport him. And an IV line. If there were any other injuries, Mickey could be losing blood internally and his blood pressure would have to be maintained with fluids to help keep an adequate level of oxygenation to his brain. He could also need a rapid drug response if he showed any signs of developing seizures.

'You know he's got spina bifida, don't you?'

'Yes.'

'And that he's got some background hydrocephalus that could be an issue with head trauma?'

No. Tom hadn't known that but a malfunction in the circulation of cerebral spinal fluid was a common complication of a defect like spina bifida. Simon had clearly had a more in-depth conversation about Mickey than Tom had ever had with Emma.

He couldn't afford to think about what else

they might have discussed. And it didn't matter. Nothing mattered except taking the best possible care of this child and getting him to hospital as quickly as possible.

'Start hyperventilating him with the bag mask,' he instructed Josh. 'I'm going to intubate.' He looked at Simon. 'Can you give me a hand? I could do with your expertise in keeping his neck stabilised.'

'Of course. I'll do whatever you need.'

He sounded concerned, Tom registered as he swiftly gathered the gear he needed. His laryngoscope, a catheter mount for the bag-mask unit, suction apparatus, artery forceps, syringe and an uncuffed endotracheal tube. A very small one.

Not the concern of a parent exactly but, then, Tom was functioning purely as a professional right now as well. Somehow he was keeping a lid on the well of emotion of how he felt about Mickey as a person and not a patient.

He managed to continuing doing that until they reached the waiting trauma team at the hospital. Until his tiny patient had been transferred to the overly large bed in Resus 1 and a crowd of specialist medical personnel and equipment produced a barrier that effectively removed him from the case.

And then it hit Tom with such a jolt he could feel the sting of tears in his eyes. He turned blindly towards a corner of the resus area in order to collect himself, but he had to stop when he felt the pressure of a soft touch on his arm.

'Tom?' Emma's voice was a shaky whisper. 'Thank you.'

Tom forced the moisture from his eyes by screwing them so tightly shut it was painful. Then he was able to look at Emma, having gathered the strength he knew she would need to lean on.

But she didn't look at him for more than a heartbeat. Her gaze was dragged back to the fragmented view of her son available between the bustling figures of the trauma team and the equipment they needed.

And one of the key people in that team was Simon.

Neurosurgeon.

Mickey's father.

* * *

There was too much happening.

Too many emotions.

Emma's head felt like a spin-drier. She was watching her thoughts through a window as they were tossed and turned but she stood apart. In a numb place that was surrounded by some kind of protective force field.

Fear was the biggest item in that mix. Horror, even, that this could have happened. That summoning the courage to try and make a new life for both herself and Mickey could actually end in such unimaginable disaster.

Tom was in there, too. More than once. There was the relief Emma had felt when she had seen it had been Tom leading the crew on the ambulance James's mother had called in desperate panic moments after Mickey's fall. If Emma could have wished for anyone to be taking the first steps in trying to save her son's life, Tom would have been that person.

Simon would also have been chosen—to at least be present for the surgery Emma knew her son was going to need. A paediatric neurosurgeon had been summoned but Emma was grateful Simon had insisted on coming with them in the ambulance.

'Of course I'm coming,' he'd said to Emma as they'd followed the stretcher carrying Mickey's small body strapped to the orange backboard. 'Did you really think I wouldn't do everything I could to help?'

There had been comfort to be found in re-alising she hadn't been completely wrong about Simon all those years ago. He may not be the right man for her but he had never been a monster.

And she did need him right now.

Mickey needed his father.

If Simon's professional expertise was all he ever contributed to Mickey's future but it was enough to save him, then Emma would never ask for anything more. If he wanted more contact in years to come, when Mickey was old enough to make an informed choice for himself, that would be fine but the past was sorting itself into a very manageable parcel that was tossing somewhere among the tumbling mix in Emma's head.

Tom had just contributed a new impression,

too, with the look she had just caught. She could have sworn there had been a hint of tears in his eyes and the message she had received hadn't made any promises that this would be all right. Tom knew as well as she did that this could never be all right but what the eye contact did seem to convey was an offer to be there for her. A confirmation that she could depend on him.

As if she hadn't already known that!

It was the one emotion that Emma would have liked to really connect with. She wanted to pull that glance out and wrap it around herself like a warm blanket but there was no point trying. She knew the force field wasn't going to allow connection.

Instead, Emma wound her own arms tightly around herself as she stood well out of the way in the best-equipped resuscitation area the emergency department had to offer. She stood frozen, inside and out, and let the snatches of what she was seeing and hearing roll over her, like a badly made, stuttering home movie that she couldn't focus on enough to follow the story.

'Systolic blood pressure dropping. Down to 80.'

'Oxygen saturation dropping. Eighty-three.'

'Is that arterial line in yet?'

'Let's get the head tilt up to thirty degrees.' That was Simon's voice. 'We can decrease ICP that way without altering CPP.'

'What's his weight? I'm just drawing up some mannitol.'

'Look out! He's seizing!'

Emma had to close her eyes at that point. She might have swayed on her feet had Tom not stepped in behind her and taken a grip on her shoulders due the sudden increase in tension in the room as anti-convulsant medications were hurriedly ordered and administered.

The comforting pressure of his hands vanished not long after that, as Mickey was moved for the urgent CT scan he needed to identify the exact nature of his head injury. It was Simon who was there to help her then. To make sure she understood what the paediatric neurosurgeon had to say when he arrived to review the results. Both he and Simon seemed to understand how numb she was and spoke to her as the frightened parent she was and not as a colleague in the medical profession.

'This is the main injury,' the surgeon said. 'A depressed occipital fracture. What we'll have to do is lift the bone piece that's pressing on Mickey's brain. There's a small tear in the tissue underneath and we'll repair that and take out the blood that's accumulated.'

'There's some bruising here…and here…' The surgeon clicked the mouse, bringing up the series of scan images on the computer screen in rapid succession. 'But they don't look like too much of a problem. Rising ICP will be the main issue—that's the pressure inside Mickey's skull.'

'It's a closed box, essentially,' Simon added. 'When pressure builds up, it compresses the brain and causes damage.'

Emma nodded. She knew that. 'Will the fact that Mickey's got spina bifida made a difference to the outcome?'

'Any extra fluid is going to add pressure but, basically, it becomes part of the same picture so it shouldn't make a difference in an acute situation like this.'

'It might have more of an impact later.' The paediatric surgeon was about the same age as Simon and he had a kind smile. 'It'll be months before the risk of even a small fall becomes acceptable and Mickey might need some protective headgear for when he gets back to learning to walk. It's a major setback as far as mobility goes, I'm afraid.'

'We can cope with that.' Emma couldn't think that far ahead yet. 'How long will the surgery take?'

'Hard to say. At least a couple of hours, I expect. He'll be in Recovery for a while and then we'll get him moved to the paediatric intensive care unit. The development of acute brain swelling is the main danger we're facing. We'll be fighting that with a fair barrage of drugs. Steroids and diuretics and so on. He's also going to need pretty intensive monitoring so you can expect to see a lot of lines in place, including an ICP probe and a urinary catheter. You OK with all that?'

'Emma's a nurse,' Simon said. 'I'm sure she's got a good idea of what she can expect.'

'Just look after him, please,' Emma whispered. 'Do the best you can.'

'Of course.' The surgeon gripped her shoulder briefly. 'I'd be stupid to tell you not worry too much but remember that we're all on your side. On Mickey's side.'

Emma was taken to the relatives' room and a nurse stayed with her. It was then that she realised how much worse this all was because Tom was not nearby any more. She hadn't thought to ask for his company in the stress of moving Mickey to CT and now he'd been left well behind.

Maybe he'd had to go out on another call. Emma had no idea of the time any more. Of when Tom's shift might be due to finish or when Mickey might come out from the ominous space that the operating theatre represented.

The passage of time also seemed to be on the other side of that protective shield.

It had ceased to matter.

* * *

Tom had never checked his watch so often.

He hung around for as long as he could in the emergency department, fussing over paperwork and cleaning gear, hoping for some news about Mickey's CT scan.

'We really need to get back to base,' Josh finally said.

'Control knows where we are. I need to find out what's happening with Mickey.'

'Do you want to stay? Maybe you should be up there with Emma.'

He should. Of course he should. But Emma hadn't said anything about wanting him to be with her. What had happened between her and Simon prior to the dreadful accident? What understandings might have been reached regarding Simon's involvement in Mickey's life? In *Emma's* life?

And Simon was the person she needed with her at the moment. He was the one who was in a position to really help Mickey and that was what mattered the most.

'I'll come back as soon as we're off duty,' Tom told Josh. 'It's only a couple of hours away. It might take that long to get Mickey to Theatre in the first place and it'll be a whole lot longer before he gets out.'

Josh gave him a sympathetic, light punch on his shoulder. 'Maybe you should take tomorrow off. You won't be a whole lot of use at work when you're this worried, mate.'

Tom nodded slowly. What excuse had Emma given that time she'd run away from work due to emotional stress? A family emergency?

That was what he was facing now. This was a crisis. And Emma and Mickey were his family.

Or they would be, if there was anything Tom could do to influence the winds of fate.

He found Emma in the relatives' waiting area adjacent to Theatre. She was sitting so still and looking so drained that all Tom wanted to do was to gather her into his arms.

Something made him hesitate. The quiet greeting and look Tom received advertised a distance to Emma he'd never sensed before. It felt like he was looking at the shell of the woman he loved, sitting there, and the real

Emma was locked away somewhere he couldn't touch.

Why?

Did she not want him there? Had she already started the process of disengaging from their relationship because she'd had an offer that was so much better—for Mickey, if not herself?

Tom might have tried to push gently through that barrier anyway but for the curious gaze of the nurse in the room and the fact that Simon entered the waiting area just after Tom.

The surgeon was still wearing the disposable head covering and bootees required for Theatre and his mask dangled with only the top string having been snapped clear.

'We're nearly there,' he informed Emma. 'It's all gone as well as we could have hoped. Intracranial pressure is within normal limits and all vital signs are stable. You'll be able to see him soon.'

Emma nodded at Simon but didn't smile.

Simon nodded at Tom as he left the room again. He wasn't smiling either.

Tom sat down beside Emma. It was a poor

second best to take hold of her hand instead of her whole body, but the feeling of being shut out and helpless was even stronger now and touching Emma was a hell of a lot better than doing nothing at all.

Tom could understand why everyone was so grim. He had never felt less like smiling himself in his whole life.

Mickey came out of Theatre, his head swathed in bandages, looking tiny and fragile among all the high-tech monitoring equipment attached to him with a spaghetti of wires and tubing.

His surgeon was as satisfied as Simon had been with the procedure and he explained it all carefully to Emma as she stood beside her son's bed in Recovery, still holding Tom's hand like an anchor.

'We'll make arrangements for you to stay with Mickey in the ICU.' The surgeon gave Tom a curious glance. 'Are there any other relatives you'd like me to talk to? His father, perhaps?'

So Simon hadn't mentioned the connection

He had made his choice about the level of involvement he wanted in Mickey's life and apparently it was only going to be professional at this point in time.

Emma shook her head in answer to the question but somewhere inside herself, she was nodding. They would be OK.

Did she mean herself and Mickey? Herself and Tom? All three of them? Emma couldn't have said what she meant or even whether her statement held any degree of accuracy. She only knew that she didn't need Simon to be in her life long term. Neither did Mickey. In that sense, they *would* be OK.

The past was well and truly dealt with.

The present had become a blur.

Night and day merged in the artificial environment of an intensive care unit that lacked any windows in the cubicle Mickey occupied. A comfortable armchair was provided for Emma and occasionally she dozed, overcome by exhaustion. And fear.

Sometimes Tom wasn't there when she

woke but a lot of the time he was. Conversation was minimal. Often he simply held her hand, sharing her vigil. As the friend he'd been from almost the first moment they'd met. It was a weird way to be together. Impersonal in some ways and intimate in others. They were never really alone and Tom gave no hint of wanting to be anything more than a friend and support. And that was precisely what Emma needed. She didn't have the emotional energy to think of anything other than Mickey.

Her world shrank to the parameters defined by the monitoring equipment. The only news she was interested in were the numbers flashing on numerous displays recording the level of oxygen saturation, pressure levels within Mickey's skull, heart and respiration rates and much more.

Other bulletins were brought by staff members when each new set of lab results came in.

'Blood glucose is stable again.'

'Renal function is looking good.'

'No sign of any infection and his temperature had dropped so that's good.'

The daily routine of caring for Mickey gave welcome bursts of gentle activity. It was Emma who washed her son, put artificial tears in his eyes and helped keep an accurate fluid balance of what went into his small body and what came out.

Weaning him from the ventilator took up much of the second day but seeing him breathe for himself gave Emma real hope. As the levels of sedation decreased, she waited for her son to wake up.

But he remained deeply unconscious and responsive only to painful stimuli.

'He might be able to hear us,' Emma said to Tom, 'mightn't he?'

'I reckon. Keep talking to him, Em. And I'll bring his books in. We can read his favourite stories.'

And they did. They read to him. They talked to him. Emma even sang songs softly.

A barrage of specialist tests was ordered the next day, including a repeat CT scan. The results all seemed good and Mickey's doctors looked puzzled.

'There's no obvious reason for his continuing coma,' Emma was told. 'Everything we've checked is looking better than we could have hoped for at this stage. It might just be a matter of being a little more patient.'

The next scheduled review by the whole team was the following morning. Tom was there again by the time the entourage of surgeons, their registrars and Mickey's nurses gathered. The cubicle was crowded. Silence fell as they finished discussing the latest improvements all the equipment and tests revealed.

And then it happened.

Mickey opened his eyes.

His bewildered gaze found his mother first. Then Tom. It moved slowly, paused briefly at the sight of Simon and then Mickey closed his eyes again.

Emma's fingers flew to touch his face gently.

'Mickey? Are you awake, darling? Can you open your eyes again?'

Eyelids flickered but didn't open.

'Tired, Mummy,' Mickey mumbled. 'Want to sleep.'

A collective sigh of relief was felt rather than heard around Emma. Mickey was not only regaining consciousness, he could speak intelligibly and he had recognised his mother.

They couldn't ask for anything more right now.

Everybody was smiling. Especially Emma, even as she reached for a handful of tissues to mop her tears.

CHAPTER TEN

ASPECTS of the world outside the hospital walls assumed increasing importance as Mickey improved steadily over the next few days and settled after his transfer from Intensive Care into a side room of the general paediatric ward.

Some things were a worry. Like the realisation that Emma had completely forgotten her promise to Phoebe to care for her cat and pot plants.

'It wasn't a problem,' Tom assured her. 'Mum took care of all that. She was glad there was something she could do to help. She'd love to come and visit Mickey when he's feeling a bit better, too.'

He *was* feeling much better.

'I want to go *home,*' he informed Emma.

'Not just yet,' Emma responded. 'We need a few more days here so everybody can look after that poor head of yours.'

Where was 'home' going to be, in any case?

'You have to come back,' Emma's mother said firmly, when her parents caught up on the news of Mickey's recovery. 'I don't think New Zealand is a good place for either of you. Bad things come in threes, you know.'

But Emma had already counted, thanks to growing up with her mother's superstitions. The accident with the van had been the first bad thing and that hadn't been entirely without a silver lining because that had been how they'd met Tom.

Mickey's accident had been the third…and last, because the second bad thing had been the rift between Tom and herself.

And she still hadn't found a way to mend it. Not that there was any negative tension between them now. How could there be when Tom had just spent virtually all of his four days off at the hospital with Mickey? He had shown that he cared in so many ways.

It had been Tom who had made and fielded the numerous phone calls from Britain and Australia to keep all interested parties up to date with events and progress. He brought food and coffee and clean clothes for Emma and toys and books for Mickey. He never seemed to tire of reading stories but his most valued contribution as far as Mickey was concerned was the framed photograph of Mickey standing beside Max. It held pride of place on his bedside locker.

Tom was back in the role of being a best friend. Emma was sure it wouldn't have been that hard for them to find a few minutes alone. She had even suggested it, her heart in her mouth, a couple of days ago.

'I could do with a bit of fresh air,' she'd said—failing to keep her tone as casual as she'd intended. 'Fancy a walk down by the river, Tom?'

The momentary hesitation had given Mickey a chance to answer on Tom's behalf.

'No,' he said firmly. 'I want Tom to stay here.'

'But you're tired, darling. You're going to have a sleep, remember?'

'Tom can watch me.' There was a tiny waver in Mickey's voice. 'Like Max does.'

Emma wouldn't have been able to resist that unspoken plea for security from her son and Tom had smiled as he'd caught her gaze. Maybe his expression had been a little resigned. Apologetic even. But he *had* hesitated long enough for Mickey to get in first and Emma had thought she'd detected a whiff of relief as he'd raised a hand in a gesture of acquiescence. Emma had decided to forgo the walk herself but Tom's smile had broadened.

'You go,' he'd suggested. 'Enjoy. You could probably do with a bit of time to yourself in any case.'

Was Tom waiting—as he had in the days before Emma had planned that first meeting with Simon? Letting her have the space and time she might need to find out what the best course of action was for herself and therefore for Mickey? Or had he decided that the baggage she brought with her was too great a threat to a deeper and more permanent relationship?

Emma was too tentative to try asking for

time alone with Tom again. Instead, she tried to take advantage of any opportunities to reassure Tom that her baggage had been dealt with. Shaken out and repacked and put into storage. That she was absolutely clear about where she wanted her future to be.

With Tom.

Most of those opportunities were limited to dropping hints into conversation. Like the time Tom's visit coincided with Simon's exit from Mickey's room.

'He was just here to check up on progress,' Emma told Tom. 'He may not have done the surgery himself but he's been keeping a very careful eye on everything.'

'He's been great.' Tom sounded almost enthusiastic. 'I suspect I misjudged the man. You couldn't have had better support.'

'But I have,' Emma's response was swift. 'Simon only comes in for a couple of minutes here and there, Tom. Purely on a professional basis. It's you that's been my rock.'

'It's what friends are for,' he said lightly.

He'd said that when he'd offered to share

his house with Emma and Mickey. To share his life. Was that the level their relationship had returned to? Where it was doomed to stay?

It wasn't nearly enough.

But what if Tom wasn't as sure as she was? If *he* needed the time and space to decide what was best for himself? Emma might ruin things by seeming to put him under pressure. And what if he rejected her?

That was what was really holding her back. Now that Emma didn't have to face the fear of losing her son, the fear of losing Tom was looming larger every day.

And Emma needed time to gather the inner strength that this latest life crisis had exhausted. If Tom didn't want them in his life, Emma was nowhere near ready to find out yet.

The final IV line was removed from Mickey's arm the following day and Simon was part of the team that came to subject Mickey to a very thorough reassessment.

He had a bright light shone into his eyes. His ears were peered into for long enough to elicit impatience.

'Ouch,' Mickey protested, even though it didn't hurt.

He had as full a neurological check as was possible for a patient who would not be allowed on his feet for some time yet. He wiggled toes and fingers, squeezed hands, tracked objects with his eyes and responded with increasing firmness to a pinprick test.

'Ouch!'

The bandage was removed from his head and the surgical site carefully assessed. Emma was relieved to see that Mickey's soft black curls hadn't been shaved. Without the bandage, he suddenly looked far more like her little boy. Even the awful bruising that had come out around his eyes was fading now.

The paediatric surgeon was clearly enjoying talking to Mickey as he made his examination. It wasn't just a test for speech clarity or memory.

'Do you like being in New Zealand?' he asked towards the end.

'Yes. I do.'

'What's the best bit?'

'Max.'

'Who's Max?'

'He's my friend.'

'My dog,' Tom put in, from where he was quietly observing the examination along with Emma. 'That's a photo of him with Mickey on his locker.'

'Wow! He's huge.'

'He looks after me,' Mickey said. 'He even watches when I'm asleep.'

Emma caught the look that Simon sent in Tom's direction. An assessing kind of glance. Was Simon wondering whether Tom was a suitable candidate as a father figure to his biological child?

He caught Emma's gaze immediately afterwards. *Yes,* she tried to communicate.

No one could make a better father than Tom.

Eventually, the visit concluded with an almost clean bill of health for Mickey.

'Miraculous the way some kids can bounce back from something like this,' the surgeon said cheerfully. 'We'll need to keep a careful eye on him for a while yet but I think in a few months' time you won't even know it ever happened.' He looked at his colleague. 'Did you want to see anyone else on our rounds this morning, Simon?'

'You're happy if I discharge Paige today?'

'Absolutely. Yesterday's scan didn't show any evidence of residual tumour, did it? And she's walking without her crutches now.'

'I'll catch up with you in a few minutes and we'll see her then.'

'Sure.'

Mickey's surgeon left, and the registrars followed. They closed the door of the side room behind them and Mickey was left with only three adults in his room. Emma, Tom and…Simon.

There was a moment's awkward silence and then Simon cleared his throat.

'I'm heading overseas again tomorrow,' he said. 'I've got a couple of days in the States where I'm going to sign a contract on that position I've been offered. I'm only coming back here in order to work out my notice. Is there anything more you'd like me to do for you and Mickey before I go, Emma?'

Emma smiled as she shook her head. 'You've been wonderful, Simon. I've felt much happier knowing that you were part of the care Mickey's been given. Thank you so much.'

Simon shot a brief glance towards Tom and then shifted on his feet. He looked far less the confident consultant than he had just minutes ago.

'It was a real surprise seeing you again, Emma. I'd like to wish you all the best for everything. It's been a pleasure to meet Mickey as well. He's…ah…a credit to you.'

'Thanks.' Emma smiled again. 'He's a credit to himself, really. You're pretty special, aren't you, sweetheart?'

Mickey ignored the question. He was watching Simon suspiciously.

'I don't like you,' he informed the surgeon.

'No?' Simon looked even more disconcerted. 'You might change your mind one day. I like *you*.'

Emma was holding her breath, having closed her eyes at the wince Mickey's statement had evoked. She opened them to look cautiously at her son. Mickey had no memory of the fall from the climbing frame but did he remember the conversation about his real father? His name? The fact that Simon and Emma had been engrossed in talking to each other when he'd seen them together in the playground that day?

Mickey transferred his gaze to Tom and the frown lines disappeared from his small face.

'I like *Tom,*' he announced. 'I want *him* to be my daddy.'

Emma's nerve endings seemed to catch alight with a sharp tingle of alarm. She would never have planned to bring things out into the open so blatantly. Especially not with both Tom and Simon in the same room.

Her future was hanging in the balance here. The air was suddenly charged with unleashed energy. An emotional bomb that was ticking rather loudly.

She tried, and failed, to take a deep, calming breath.

'That's fine by me,' Simon was saying gravely to Mickey.

Three pairs of eyes swivelled automatically to where Tom was standing, looking slightly dazed by the turn in the conversation. The fact that some input was clearly expected from him took a second or two to sink in. Then he mirrored the example set by Simon's earlier discomfort and he cleared his throat.

'I…ah…it's fine by me, too,' he said finally to Mickey, 'but it rather depends on what Mummy thinks about it all, doesn't it?'

It was Emma's turn to feel the intense scrutiny.

The expectation.

The *hope*.

She held Tom's gaze for a long moment. Not that she was consciously hesitating in any way. She just wanted to revel in what she saw in those dark eyes.

The love.

The promise of a future together.

A whole family.

Her lips curved into a smile of pure joy.

'It's fine by me, too,' Emma said softly. 'A whole lot better than fine, in fact.'

* * *

Or was it?

Tom seemed very quiet after Simon had left. He read Mickey a story but then said he needed a bit of fresh air.

Emma followed him out of Mickey's room.

'Tom? What's wrong?'

He turned and waited for Emma to catch up, standing calmly to one side of the corridor and seemingly oblivious to the normal traffic of a ward's central passageway at that time of the day. Nursing staff were bustling past, parents walked up and down, some carrying children or babies, children went past—in wheelchairs, on crutches, on foot and even crawling.

It was noisy and busy and that, in fact, gave two people all they needed to hold a quietly private conversation.

'I'm sorry you were put on the spot like that, Em.'

Emma felt a chill at his words. Had Tom said what he had so as not to disappoint Mickey? Did he think she had simply been playing along? Had what she'd thought she'd seen in his eyes been the result of wishful thinking on her part?

'I wasn't put on the spot,' she said firmly. 'Not like that. OK, it was a bit embarrassing to do it in front of Simon, but he already knew how I felt about you. I wasn't sure that you did and I was getting too nervous to say anything so I'm *glad* Mickey brought things to a head.' Emma caught her bottom lip between her teeth. 'I'm sorry if you felt pressured. I wouldn't hold you to anything you weren't comfortable with. Mickey will just have to…' The rest of her words were drowned out by the rattle of a meal trolley being wheeled past.

Tom raised his voice. 'The only thing I wouldn't be comfortable with, Emma White,' he said, 'is the thought of the rest of my life without you and Mickey in it.'

'Really?' Seeds of doubt vanished before they had even taken root. 'You really meant that you want to be Mickey's dad?'

Tom shook his head and Emma's heart sank like a stone. But then Tom smiled. A real smile. One of those wonderful smiles like the one he'd given her that day in the van.

'Actually, what I want more than anything is to be your husband,' he said. 'Being Mickey's dad is an unexpected bonus.'

Emma gaped. It was one thing to be given the promise of a potential future together. It was quite another to find she might be receiving a proposal of marriage!

'This is hardly the most romantic venue.' Tom eyed a child with a rather nasty rash who'd stopped to stare at them with great interest until his attention was taken by the approaching cleaner wielding a large mop. 'But I don't think I can wait any longer. I love you, Emma—more than I thought it was possible to love anyone. Will you marry me? Please?'

The cleaner was moving at speed. Emma found a mop aiming for her feet. The woman grinned at Emma. 'Don't let me interrupt, love,' she instructed. 'I'd say yes if I was you. He's got a nice smile.'

Tom had the best smile in the world. And

Emma had no intention of saying anything but yes. Or maybe she did.

'Of course I'll marry you,' she said. 'I love you, too, Tom.'

For the first time since Mickey had been admitted, Emma left the hospital grounds that night after he'd fallen asleep.

She went home. With Tom.

Where she belonged.

Being in his bed, in his arms, had never been so wonderful. There was a new depth that could only have been added by the stress of recent events and by the absolute closure of any space between them engendered by that rift.

Tom pulled Emma a little closer, which she would have thought impossible the way their bodies were still entwined in the aftermath of their love-making.

'Do you know, it was the first time I heard you laugh that I really fell in love with you?'

'I think I fell in love with you the first time I saw you smile,' Emma replied. 'Except I con- vinced myself that I was just really grateful for everything you'd done for us and that you were a really kind person and I shouldn't read anything more into it.'

'You couldn't afford to read any more into it until you knew where you stood with Simon. Things were already complicated enough.'

'No. I think I was just blind.' Emma snuggled happily in Tom's arms and sighed with deep contentment. 'Not any more, though. Mickey could see it all along.'

'See what?'

'That there wasn't any good reason for you not to be his father.'

She could feel Tom smiling in the darkness. His tone was as contented as Emma felt.

'He did sound pretty sure, didn't he? About who he wanted for a daddy?'

'He sure did.'

'We'll look after him together, Em. He'll get through all this and then there won't be any stopping that young man.'

There wasn't. Mickey made such a good recovery after his head injury that his surgeon relented on the time frame to let him become mobile again and three months later he was in an intensive physiotherapy programme, with Phoebe cheering him on.

Six months later, he was walking without crutches. He would still need callipers for a while yet but he wasn't bothered.

The long trousers he got to wear to his mum's wedding hid the walking aids in any case. And Max was there beside him, with a big white ribbon around his neck, just in case Mickey needed any support.

Phoebe was a bridesmaid and she looked just as proud as Emma when Mickey stepped forward with the little velvet cushion that had the rings on top of it, because he managed to carry out the task without tipping them off and it had taken a lot of practice to get his balance that good.

Tom's mother had a very damp handkerchief clutched in her hand and told anyone who wanted to listen that, while Mickey would always be her first grandchild, she couldn't help but be *very* excited that he was going to have a sibling next year. She was hoping it would be a little sister.

And the bride and groom? For the most part, they had eyes only for each other and everybody who attended that ceremony smiled when they talked about it.

'They're just so in love with each other,' they invariably finished by saying.

'It was magic.'

Tom and Emma had known that all along.

MEDICAL™

Large Print

Titles for the next six months...

October

HIS VERY OWN WIFE AND CHILD Caroline Anderson
THE CONSULTANT'S NEW-FOUND FAMILY Kate Hardy
CITY DOCTOR, COUNTRY BRIDE Abigail Gordon
THE EMERGENCY DOCTOR'S DAUGHTER Lucy Clark
A CHILD TO CARE FOR Dianne Drake
HIS PREGNANT NURSE Laura Iding

November

A BRIDE FOR GLENMORE Sarah Morgan
A MARRIAGE MEANT TO BE Josie Metcalfe
DR CONSTANTINE'S BRIDE Jennifer Taylor
HIS RUNAWAY NURSE Meredith Webber
THE RESCUE DOCTOR'S BABY Dianne Drake
MIRACLE
EMERGENCY AT RIVERSIDE HOSPITAL Joanna Neil

December

SINGLE FATHER, WIFE NEEDED Sarah Morgan
THE ITALIAN DOCTOR'S PERFECT FAMILY Alison Roberts
A BABY OF THEIR OWN Gill Sanderson
THE SURGEON AND THE SINGLE MUM Lucy Clark
HIS VERY SPECIAL NURSE Margaret McDonagh
THE SURGEON'S LONGED-FOR BRIDE Emily Forbes

MILLS & BOON®
Pure reading pleasure

0907 LP 2P P1 Medical

MEDICAL™

 *Large Print*

January

February

March

MILLS & BOON®
Pure reading pleasure